SHUTTERBUGS AND CAR THIEVES

BY HILARY MILTON

WANDERER BOOKS
Published by Simon & Schuster, New York

Copyright © 1981 by Hilary Milton
All rights reserved
including the right of reproduction
in whole or in part in any form
Published by WANDERER BOOKS
A Simon & Schuster Division of
Gulf & Western Corporation
Simon & Schuster Building
1230 Avenue of the Americas
New York, New York 10020

Manufactured in the United States of America
10 9 8 7 6 5 4 3 2 1

WANDERER and colophon are trademarks of Simon & Schuster

Also available in Julian Messner Certified Edition

Library of Congress Cataloging in Publication Data
Milton, Hilary H.
Shutterbugs and car thieves.
"A Wanderer book."
Summary: When three thirteen-year-old friends discover a stolen car ring,
one is captured by the thieves and it is up to the others to save him and
expose the criminals.
[1. Crime and criminals—Fiction] I. Title.
PZ7.M6447Sh   [Fic]   81–7578
ISBN 0–671–44415–8   AACR2

To a good friend and special editor—Wendy Barish

Contents

Chapter One

Young Scott Hamner pushed aside the last clump of brush and stepped clear of the shallow forest. He stopped there and stared across a wide, weed-strewn field that had once been a thriving farm. The field stretched three or maybe four hundred yards, Scott couldn't be sure, and ended abruptly at a line of thick oak and sycamore trees.

He turned about. "Hey," he called out, "come on."

Almost immediately his two companions joined him. Jimbo Parks, Scott's next-door neighbor, had picked up a long, twisted stick that he brandished like a battling warrior. "A ready-made sword," he said, brushing away the small cockleburs that had attached themselves to his jeans.

Ellie Whittington took three steps past him, making

9

certain she was well out of the way of the weapon. She laughed and ran her fingers through her flowing black hair. "Now all you need is a fire-eating dragon."

"Yeah," Jimbo said, pretending to jab at such a beast. He made a swipe back in the direction of the forest, then turned to Scott. "Did you get a picture of that squirrel?"

Three days earlier, on Scott's thirteenth birthday, his father had given him a very small camera equipped with a new zoom lens, and that was the reason for their trek through the fields this afternoon. "Yeah, I think so. But I was hoping maybe we could find a deer."

"A deer?" Ellie wrinkled her nose. "Not any deer out in weather like this." She gave her head a little toss. "My uncle says wild animals find deep woods and lots of shade when it's hot." Like Scott, Ellie was thirteen, and both were a year older than Jimbo. Ellie's home was somewhere in Louisiana—Baton Rouge, Scott thought she'd said—but she was spending the last three weeks before school started with Jimbo and his family.

Jimbo hoisted the stick-sword and swished it through the air. "I wish we could find a bear, though—man! That'd be something to take a picture of!"

"Yeah. Well, I don't want any bears," Scott said, "but let's cross the field to the river," and he pointed to the line of thick trees.

"Okay," Ellie said, "but let's find a path—I don't like all those stickers."

Scott glanced to the left, hesitated a moment, then

pointed in that direction. "Looks like an abandoned road of some sort. Maybe it'll get us there easier."

The abandoned path, however, didn't cross the field as they'd expected. Instead, it kept to the edge of the planted pine forest they'd just walked through. After several minutes of following the path, Jimbo stopped and gazed around. "It's not crossing the field. I think it's just going to that old farmhouse."

Scott glanced ahead, paused, and raised his camera. "Hey—well, okay, then. We'll just take some pictures of it. Dad's won more prizes with photographs of fences and rotting trees than anything else."

"Who cares about an old house?" Jimbo grunted. Then he laughed easily and looked at Ellie. "Maybe he ought to go home with you and take a picture of that castle."

"What castle?" Scott asked.

"It's not really a castle," Ellie said. "It's just an old house that nobody lives in."

"But, man, it's big," Jimbo said. He strutted to the path's edge and made another swipe with the sword. "Back when it was new, I bet people were always having sword fights."

Scott glanced at his redheaded friend and laughed softly. "And you'd like to do that, wouldn't you?"

Jimbo lowered the stick, shaking his head. "Not me. If I've got to fight anybody, I'd want more than a sword to use."

"Hey," Ellie interrupted him, her voice suddenly

sounding cautious, "this road's not really abandoned."

"Yeah?" Jimbo lowered his stick. "How d'you know?"

"Look," she said, pointing to the ground. "Car tracks."

Scott stared at the packed surface, then bent down and ran his fingers over it. "You're right. Something's been over this path recently."

"Like today," Jimbo guessed. "Look." He pointed to a clear tire impression. "And it wasn't a car, either. Double tracks. Like maybe a big truck."

"But what would a truck be doing here?" Scott stood and aimed the camera down, as if fresh tire tracks on the old path might be an interesting subject for him to photograph.

"Now you're just plain wasting film," Jimbo said. "Hey, I've got an idea. When we get to the old farmhouse, why don't you take a picture of Ellie on the porch? You know, one of those sad-like things."

"Shhh," Ellie said suddenly.

"Yeah—what is it?" Jimbo's voice abruptly softened.

Scott clicked the shutter once, then stared off in the direction of the path's distant end.

"I don't know," Ellie said.

"Wait—I hear something, too," Scott said. He stood still, listening intently. "Sounds like somebody using a heavy tool."

Jimbo turned halfway around. "Well, I'm for getting out of here. Noise coming from an abandoned house spells trouble."

12

"Oh, come on," Ellie said. "You're spooking yourself." She turned to Scott. "Maybe it isn't really abandoned now."

"Well, if it's not," Jimbo said, "maybe the people there won't want company. Let's just cut across the field and find the river."

Scott aimed the camera toward the clump of trees that he believed surrounded the old farmhouse. "We can go there later," he said. "We're this close."

"Yeah," Ellie said, "and I want to know what that noise is."

"Oh," Jimbo said, stabbing at an imaginary foe, "all right. But if there's anybody home, I'm for splitting."

Five minutes later, as they rounded the turn in the path, they came abruptly onto a wide, open, dirt yard. At one side of it was the old farmhouse, abandoned and run-down as they had expected. Its wide rear porch was dirty, its posts leaning, and its slanted roof tilted badly. The other side of the yard, though, was a different matter. The huge barn was in good repair, as if it had recently been reroofed and patched. An adjoining, fenced-in lot contained no fewer than ten automobiles, two with body damage, the others in good condition. The noise Ellie had heard was coming from the barn's interior.

Scott squatted low, then motioned for Jimbo and Ellie to follow him quietly to the safety and shelter of a small shed, standing off by itself. "The barn's not abandoned," he whispered.

"Anybody can tell that," Jimbo muttered, bending low and staring around the shed's corner. "Do you know what it is they're doing?"

"I can guess," Scott said.

"What?" Ellie half stood so she could see over Jimbo.

"It's a chop shop."

"A *what*?" She looked back at Scott.

"A chop shop—I think that's what they call it," Scott repeated. "People steal cars, then tear them down for the parts."

She dropped to the ground, as if by doing so she could make herself invisible. "You—you mean that noise is coming from other people's cars being torn apart?"

"I think so," Scott said quietly.

"It's trouble, real trouble," Jimbo whispered. He turned to Scott. "Hey, how about if I go sneak a look inside?"

"You acted like you were scared a minute ago."

"I'm still scared a little," Jimbo admitted. "But I want to know how they do it."

"Maybe we'd better go now," Ellie said.

Jimbo looked to Scott. "Hey—" he caught himself, glanced toward the barn, and whispered, "I got an idea. Why don't you take the camera over there and shoot a picture?"

"Of what?"

Jimbo pointed toward the automobiles. "Those. Maybe if you got pictures and we took them to the police, they'd know what to do."

14

Ellie scratched the side of her cheek, then brushed back her long hair. "It makes sense," she said softly. "Except what if they catch you?"

Scott thought about the possible seriousness of the situation. He wasn't absolutely certain they'd come across a true chop shop—although the signs sure made it look that way. But if it was one, and if the people inside were automobile thieves, he realized that they could be in real danger if they got caught. "They wouldn't like it," he whispered. "But if we truly knew what they're doing inside—"

"I said I'd go look," Jimbo repeated, his earlier reluctance suddenly gone. He leaned forward and stared around the shed's corner. "Right there"—he made a motion toward the building's back end—"is a loose board. I'll sneak over and look in."

"Well," Scott said slowly, "but be real careful."

"And don't get caught," Ellie cautioned.

Jimbo dropped the sword-stick and got down on all fours. He hesitated a moment, then selected a path through the tall weeds, which kept him hidden until he reached the end of the barn. Scott lost sight of him when he was only a few yards away and didn't see him again until he rose up at the place where the loose board was.

Ellie could not see him at all. "What's he doing?" she asked.

"He's pushing the board aside," Scott whispered.

Luckily, the board swung back without creaking, and

Scott realized that Jimbo was able to see into the barn. "He's there now."

"I don't think it's a good idea."

"He's good at sneaking," Scott said. He thought a moment, then carefully raised his camera. Zooming in as much as he could, he aimed and snapped the shutter.

"What's that for?"

"I don't know," Scott said. "But if it's really a stolen-automobile ring, pictures'll be good."

Jimbo raised a hand, as if signaling them to come toward him. Scott relayed the idea.

"I'm not going anywhere," Ellie said. "And that little redhead's going to get us into trouble."

"Maybe he'd better come back now," Scott said. And as he put the thought into words, he felt himself getting tight and tense. His heart was racing, and he realized that they might be getting themselves into a real jam.

"Maybe you'd better call him."

"If I did and those people heard, they'd come—"

He cut his words short, for just at that moment a tall, broad-shouldered man in work overalls suddenly appeared at the far corner of the barn, not five feet from where Jimbo was crouching. He saw the young boy, hesitated only a moment, then took three quick steps and swooped down.

He grabbed Jimbo around the waist and lifted him high.

"Hey!" Jimbo was kicking both feet and flailing away

16

with both arms. "Hey—you put me down! You hear! Put me down!"

Within seconds, three other men came charging around the corner of the barn. The shortest of them, the only one not wearing work clothes, stopped abruptly. "Charlie! What the devil!"

"I caught him looking in," and the man holding Jimbo pointed to the loose board.

Scott swallowed the lump in his throat and dropped as low as he could, ducking back behind the small shed. He looked at Ellie. "They got him," he whispered. "They've got Jimbo!"

Chapter Two

As soon as the men walked back around the barn—inside, Scott figured—he caught Ellie's hand. "Come on," he whispered.

"Where?"

He pointed toward the higher weeds well in back of the barn and to a clump of small trees just beyond a low mound. "I don't think Jimbo'll tell them we're here," he said. "But they may come looking anyway."

"I don't want to leave him."

"We won't," Scott reassured her. "But we can't help him if they catch us, too."

Keeping low and staying in the tall weeds, they crept their way to a new sanctuary fifty yards from the barn. In the midst of the clump of wild plum trees, Scott rose halfway and turned to stare toward the old building. "They must have him in there with them."

"Wonder what they'll do with him."

"I don't know. But as soon as it's safe, I'll go see."

Ellie slumped to the ground and tried to peer around the small tree trunks. "Maybe they'll tie him up." She took a deep breath. "Maybe it would be better to go get the police."

"It would," Scott said. "But as soon as we left, they'd get in the truck and take him somewhere else. And we wouldn't know where."

"Do you really think they'd take him? Kidnap him?"

"I don't know. That's one reason I'm not leaving. But I also want to take some pictures of those men."

"You're crazy. How?"

"Through the loose board Jimbo pried open."

"Don't!" Ellie's voice was almost frantic. "If they catch you, too, I'll be lost."

Scott touched her arm gently. "Don't be afraid," he said quietly. "I won't get caught."

Together, they remained huddled in the plum thicket for what Scott believed to be half an hour. And when he thought the men might be concentrating on Jimbo, he set the camera and turned to Ellie. "I'll crawl over to the barn and look in—"

"They'll see you. I just know they'll see you."

"I don't think so. They'll be trying to decide what to do with Jimbo."

"All right. But don't be gone long."

Scott reassured her that he'd return soon. Then he began the long crawl to the barn. At the edge of the weeds, just short of the narrow clearing around the old structure, he stopped and strained to hear what the men were saying inside.

"What was he doing out there, anyway?" That voice sounded like the one belonging to the man called Charlie, who'd caught Jimbo.

"No telling." That was the voice of the little man in street clothes, the one Scott supposed was the boss. "But whatever he meant to do, we can't turn him loose."

"Hey, you better untie me! My daddy's not going to like it if you keep me tied up like this."

Jimbo's words sent Scott's heart racing. He glanced once over his shoulder to make certain Ellie hadn't tried to follow him. Then he hunched down as low as he could and continued his crawl to the barn wall. Gingerly, he caught the loose plank Jimbo had worked free and eased it farther back. When he had it far enough out of the way to allow himself a good view, he stopped and again looked all around. Neither of the two other men came out, and he guessed that they were busy doing whatever they'd been doing when Charlie first spotted Jimbo.

He bent over, careful not to disturb another board, and peered inside.

His eyes widened. The outside of the old building looked like any ordinary barn, but inside was a different story. Along the walls were carefully arranged stacks of automobile body parts—doors, fenders, hoods, grills, tires, and all sorts of wheels. At the opposite end were assorted engines, all looking like new. And overhead, a heavy-duty block and tackle device was suspended from a huge rail. That, he supposed, was the machine they used to remove engines.

In the center of the barn, with its rear end facing Scott, a long stake-bed truck was almost fully loaded. As he stared at it, he realized that some of the space on the truck was taken up with auto parts but in the center was a complete, almost new automobile that looked as if it had just been painted. He squinted his eyes and tried to make out the letters on its back—450SL. He swallowed. *That* was a Mercedes, an expensive Mercedes.

"I said you'd better untie me and let me go."

Scott's attention shifted quickly to the source of the voice. Jimbo was tied hand and foot, placed in a sitting position near a supporting wooden beam and held there by a stack of tires.

The man in street clothes was standing over Jimbo. "Kid," he said, "I'm asking you again—what were you doing out there?"

"Mister, I wasn't doing anything but looking. But if you don't untie me and let me go, my daddy's coming after you and he'll catch you because he's the chief of police."

Scott knew Jimbo was frightened and he guessed most any other boy would be whimpering. Not Jimbo. He'd yell and struggle and tug at the ropes, but one thing he wasn't—he wasn't a crybaby.

"What's your name, kid?"

"None of your business."

"You say your old man's chief of police?"

"That's what I said and you'd better believe me, too."

The only police work Mr. Parks had ever done, Scott thought, was serving as a crossing guard at school three years earlier, when the Bremerton police force went on strike. He owned a men's clothing store, with three locations—one downtown and the other two at shopping centers. But that was typical of Jimbo—he'd try anything once, say almost anything if he thought it would get him out of trouble. Like the time when they were in the fourth grade and old Miss Wilkens said he was trying to look over Nancy Cater's shoulder for test answers. Jimbo had loudly proclaimed his innocence, assuring the teacher that he'd been having chills and eye trouble for over a week.

The street-clothed man turned to Charlie, his hand on his hip. "I don't like it—I don't like it at all. If we let him go, you know he'll call the cops."

Charlie scratched the side of his head. "I don't know, Dave. A kid who talks as much as this one, likely nobody'd believe him."

The two other men were now busy placing automobile body parts on the truck, taking pains that nothing touched the sides of the Mercedes. As they worked, they gradually pulled a huge tarpaulin over the front of the car, also covering the pieces they'd loaded.

Jimbo struggled and tugged against the ropes. "I mean it, whoever you are. You'd *better* let me go."

"Tell you what," the man called Dave said. "Take him with you."

"Hunh?" Charlie quit scratching. "Dave, do you know what you're saying? That's kidnapping."

"You got a better idea?"

"I got no idea at all. Except we've got to get this 450 to Columbus tonight and those parts'd better be in the Big A before daylight."

Columbus, Scott thought. And "Big A." He didn't know the distances, but he knew the men meant to drive the truck somewhere and that it would take most of the night to do it.

"All right. Then here's what we'll do. Put the kid in the cab—"

"Look, I don't want to hear his jabbering any more than I have to."

"Okay, okay. Gag him. But put him in the cab and take him to Columbus. Boot him out somewhere along the way—after you make the Columbus delivery."

"I don't like it."

"I didn't say to like it," Dave said. "But we can't leave him here, and we can't turn him loose."

Scott had heard enough. Very cautiously, he held the camera up and shot four pictures: one of the men with Jimbo, one of the other two men, one of the Mercedes, and one of the big truck. When he thought he had all he

23

could afford to take at the moment, he eased the loose board back into place and crawled back to the plum thicket.

Ellie was leaning forward, shaking all over. "I was afraid they'd caught you, too."

He shook his head. "But Jimbo's tied to a post," he said, and he described everything he'd seen.

"What're we going to do?"

"Get him out." Scott glanced toward the barn. "In a little while, they'll have the truck loaded. Then the man named Dave and probably one of the others will leave. I'm guessing Charlie and the fourth man'll take the truck."

"But how will we get Jimbo?"

Scott made a face. "I didn't see a car, but I think there's one in the barn—I couldn't see it for the truck. When the boss gets ready to leave, they'll have to open the barn door—"

"And we'll run in then?"

"No," Scott said quickly. "They'd catch us for sure. If they do like most people, they'll get the car out, then they'll stand there talking for a while. We'll slip in the back."

"No doors," Ellie said.

"That loose board's wide enough for us to crawl through. We'll slip in when they're not looking, untie Jimbo, and get out the same way."

"Maybe it won't work."

"It had better."

The sun was almost below the horizon and tree shadows were stretched over the ground when Scott heard the creak of a heavy hinge. He touched Ellie's shoulder. "You hear that?"

"Yes," she whispered.

Moments later, they heard a small automobile engine roar and whine to life. "Just as I thought," Scott said. "Come on." And without waiting for her response, he began crawling rapidly toward the back end of the barn. They were almost there when the motor was accelerated and Scott heard the distinctive sound of tires rolling slowly over bare ground.

"They're going," Ellie said.

The tire sounds ceased, and once more Scott thought the barn door was being moved. He frowned and glanced at Ellie. "I hope that wasn't the truck."

"They closed the door—maybe they all went and took Jimbo with them."

"We'll see." And again without waiting for her, Scott crawled the rest of the way to the loose board. Very cautiously, he eased it back and away from the wall, setting the end of it onto the ground without making any noise. He bent over and peered inside.

The truck was just as he'd last seen it, but Jimbo was gone. He swallowed hard and turned to motion Ellie forward. She joined him, and he pointed to the post where their friend had been tied.

"They—they took him—"

"Shhh," Scott cautioned. "Maybe not. Maybe they

just moved him somewhere else." He hesitated a moment longer to make sure none of the men had remained behind, then he gingerly worked himself through the narrow opening. Once inside the barn, he helped Ellie crawl through. He stood, then, looking all around him. "There," he said finally, pointing to the side of the truck. "Let's slip over to it."

They reached the safety of the stake-bed truck, scanned all the areas, but saw no sign of Jimbo. Then they heard a tapping sound. Scott spun about and then tiptoed his way to the truck door. Stretching himself up, he stared inside the cab.

There was Jimbo, his feet tied together, his hands bound behind his back, a white rag wrapped like a blindfold about his eyes, and a wide band of tape across his mouth. Scott tapped the window. Jimbo turned toward the sound, struggled against the ropes, but could not move.

"Jimbo!" Scott hissed, then looked quickly toward the barn door. It did not open.

Jimbo turned at the sound of Scott's voice, kicked his feet out, and tried to wriggle free. He could not.

"We'll get you," Scott whispered. He caught the door handle and attempted to turn it. It refused to budge. He tried again, and again, without success. "I'll try the other side." It, too, was locked, he discovered seconds later. The windows were closed, and when he examined them through the glass, he realized that the inside latches had been removed.

Scott turned to Ellie, shaking his head. "Locked," he muttered. "And Jimbo can't help us." He looked frantically about, hoping to find a tool he could use to break one of the panes. At that moment, however, they both heard the car's engine roar and knew the man called Dave and perhaps one of the others were leaving. Before either of them could move, the barn door began to open.

Scott grabbed Ellie's arm and pulled her toward the rear of the truck. "Get in," he said. "Hurry!"

She seemed ready to argue, but he pushed her up under the tarpaulin. Without a word, then, she clambered onto the oil-stained bed and scrambled forward. Scott sprang up after her, and together they worked their way forward. Scott caught the Mercedes's door handle, quietly opened the door, and urged her inside the vehicle. They had just settled low in the seats and cautiously shut the door when they heard two men enter.

"I don't like it—I don't like it none at all." The deep voice, Scott imagined, belonged to one of the two men who'd been loading the truck. "Mr. D. goin' off, leavin' that young'un to me an' you. Snatchin' cars is one thing—gettin' hit for a kidnappin' rap is something else again."

"Don't sweat it," Charlie said. "Look, Jake, Dave knows what he's doing. And like he said, all we got to do is drop the kid on the highway. You know—in the middle of nowhere."

"It maybe won't work."

"It'll work," Charlie said. "Folks'll figure the brat made up a story to save his hide—that's what runaway young'uns do."

"Yeah. Well, you better be right."

"I'm right. Count on it."

Ellie nudged Scott. "They're inside now," she said, "and it sounds like they'll be driving the truck real soon."

"I know," Scott whispered back.

"What'll we do?"

"What *can* we do but ride wherever they're going?"

Ellie trembled. "I don't like it."

"I don't, either. I just hope they don't think to look in here again."

Shortly after five-thirty, Louise Parks, Jimbo's mother, telephoned Alice Hamner and told her to send Jimbo and Ellie home. Learning that all three had ridden off on their bikes for an afternoon of picture taking, she laughed about it and returned to her cooking. Half an hour later, though, when Alice called back to say she was getting concerned, both mothers began phoning friends and classmates of their children. Not one, they discovered, had seen Jimbo, Scott, or Ellie.

By seven o'clock, both families were becoming truly worried. Suppers were on the stoves, staying warm but losing flavor. Darkness was settling in, and Walter Parks was all for getting in the car and driving somewhere to begin searching—though where, he wasn't certain. When the telephone rang, Louise grabbed it, just knowing the caller would be Jimbo. "Mrs. Parks,"—the voice was that of a young boy, but not Jimbo—"this is Horace Leslie. I was walking home a while ago and saw three bicycles parked by the woods. One of them looked like Jimbo's, and I thought maybe somebody had stolen it."

Louise swallowed and hurriedly took the address. "Thank you for calling, Horace—can you meet us there in about twenty minutes?"

"Yes, ma'am."

Twenty minutes later the Parks and Hamners stopped at the intersection of Grove Avenue and Duncan Drive. Horace pointed to the bikes and said, "That one looks like Jimbo's."

The green one was Jimbo's, the yellow three-speed belonged to Scott, and the old blue one was the bike Ellie had been using. The woods, they discovered, were a forty-acre pine field that separated the residential section from a large farm, one that Horace told them belonged to a Jeb Ferguson. "Except," he said, "they don't farm it now because there's lots of sinkholes all over it. And way past the farm there's a river."

Louise knew the river—the Delonga—and she didn't like the thought. "Does anybody live on the farm?" she asked.

Horace shook his head. "And don't anybody ever go there, either. It's posted because of the holes."

Louise turned to Ralph Hamner. "Do you know this area?"

He shook his head slowly. "Not as well as I wish I did."

Alice said slowly, "Scott knows better," and walked to the edge of the darkened pine field. "I think we'd better call the sheriff."

Chapter Three

Jimbo didn't like it. He didn't like it at all. Here he was, his hands and feet tied, his eyes blindfolded, and that sticky tape over his mouth. He was hungry and he was scared and he did not like the smell of oil on the two men's clothing. But most of all, he was mad—mad that they'd caught him, mad that they'd put him in the truck, and mad that the doors had been locked so Scott and Ellie couldn't get him out.

The one called Charlie was driving, and Jimbo wished he had a knife. He'd cut the ropes and stick Charlie in the leg, and while Charlie was hollering, that would be the best time to grab the keys and throw them out the window. It was against the law, kidnapping—that's what they were doing, kidnapping him. If he could throw the keys away, they'd be stuck, and sooner or later a highway patrolman would come along and arrest them.

31

"Hey, kid," Charlie's voice was louder than it had to be. "You promise you won't make any trouble and I'll take that tape off your mouth."

Jimbo made a sound, but no words came out.

"I know you can't talk. Just nod your head that you promise."

Jimbo didn't want to promise him anything, but he sure wished he could moisten his lips. He nodded vigorously.

"Well," Charlie said slowly, "Jake'll take it off. But if you yell out one time, we'll put it right back on."

This time Jimbo shook his head, indicating he would not make a sound.

"Okay, Jake—you can take it off."

Jake's hand smelled like old grease as it came close to Jimbo's face. Jimbo held his breath while the man caught the tape, pulled gently once, then jerked it off.

"Ow! That hurt, dummy!"

"Kid," Jake's voice was deep and husky, "you better watch that tongue—I don't like smarty kids calling me dummy."

"Well, it's dumb anyway. You've got no business taking me wherever you're going."

"I guess you want us to let you out, hunh?" Charlie's laugh was harsh and quick.

"You'd better let me out," Jimbo said. "I told you and I told that Dave or whatever—my daddy's the chief of police of Bremerton, and he don't like people who steal cars. Or kidnap his little boy."

Jake made a snorting sound. "Look, kid, I don't know who or what your old man is, but Lou Batson's the chief of police in Bremerton. And he ain't married—I know that for a fact."

Jimbo swallowed, touched his tongue to his lips. "Yeah—well, I guess you know that because he's probably arrested you for stealing."

Jake laughed again. "He's tried."

Jimbo wished he'd been able to unlock the doors when Scott tried to get him out. He wished he'd never crept to the barn and peeked inside. He wished they'd not even gone picture taking—Scott could have shot all the pictures he wanted right there in his own backyard. "This time, he'll catch you for sure."

"Yeah? How's that?"

"Because we got pictures." The minute the words came out, Jimbo wished he hadn't said them.

"*What* did you say?" Charlie's voice no longer had a trace of humor. "*Who* got pictures?"

Jimbo set his head forward. "Nobody," he said softly. "I just made that up—"

"You said *we*," Charlie said. "Who's *we*?"

"I didn't mean anything."

"You said *we* and you meant it. Now look, kid, we're not playing a schoolyard game. Was somebody else out there in the field?"

"I'm not telling you anything else."

"I don't like it," Jake said softly. "Ten dollars'll get you twenty that he wasn't by himself. Tell you what we'd better do—first chance we get, we'd better call Dave."

"And say what?" Charlie asked.

"Tell him maybe somebody else *was* at the barn. Tell him he'd better get some of the boys out there and clear it out. Quick."

Jimbo wished he had not said a word. He wished they'd just left the tape over his mouth. If Scott had gotten pictures, he could take them to the sheriff or somebody, maybe just to his father. They'd have the patrol out looking for this truck in no time at all.

"I guess you're right," Charlie said. "And we'll have to think of something else to do with this young'un. We can't put him out now. We can't even do it after we dump the Mercedes in Columbus."

"Yeah? Then what'll we do with him?"

"I don't know. I'll ask Dave, but he'll probably say to leave him tied up somewhere."

Jake shifted and seemed to slouch against the seat. "Man, like I said back yonder—I don't like it at all."

Jimbo thought about it and he decided he didn't like it, either.

"I thought Mercedes cars were supposed to be comfortable," Ellie said.

"They are." Scott shifted position and pushed himself away from the steering wheel. If those men just hadn't pulled the tarpaulin all the way over and covered up the vehicle, maybe he could see outside. He knew there were lots of parts surrounding them, but he knew none were touching the car's sides. Maybe he could spot a sign or a road marker—something to give them an idea of which direction they were traveling in.

"Well," Ellie said, "this one's not comfortable."

"It's the truck."

"How long are we going to stay shut up like this?"

"I don't know. But one thing's for sure, we've got to figure a way to get out. And we've got to get word to my mom and dad or to Jimbo's folks."

"How? How can we do anything when we're trapped in this car?"

"One of us will just have to get out."

Ellie turned quickly and sat forward. "Get out? You must be crazy to think of getting out while we're going down the road."

Scott thought for a moment, and slowly one hand slipped to the little camera. "And something else. If we could get these pictures developed, that could help the police capture these crooks."

"I wish somebody would capture them," Ellie said. "But there's no way."

"Maybe there is."

"How?"

Scott's hand went from the camera to the Mercedes's steering wheel, from there to the door. "I know. I'll ease out of the car and throw something out of the back. They'll hear the noise and stop to pick it up. And while they do, one of us can slip over the side."

"One of us?"

"Yes."

Ellie made a sniffing sound. "I won't like it—being left here all by myself."

"Then I'll stay—somebody's got to help Jimbo. And you can climb out. When the truck leaves, you can find a telephone somewhere."

"Well," she said slowly, "I want to get out, and that's for sure. But I don't know where we are."

"Do you have a better idea?"

Before she could answer, they felt a sudden change in the speed of the truck. Scott hunched forward, trying to see through the window. "Something's gone wrong."

"What do you mean?"

"They're stopping."

The truck seemed to coast for a short distance, then it swerved to the right, and the bumpy surface told Scott they were on the road's shoulder, or perhaps turning into a parking area. After a hundred feet or so, the truck came to a stop and the door on the driver's side opened.

"I wonder what's going on," Ellie whispered.

"I don't know. Maybe we can hear something."

Although they could see nothing because of the heavy tarpaulin, they distinctly heard a machine being jiggled and a coin being dropped into a metal slot. "Somebody wants a cold drink—"

"Shhh," Scott said. "Listen carefully."

Now they heard the distinct clicks as a telephone dial was turned. Moments later, Charlie's voice came clear as he said, "Dave, we may have trouble."

Scott stuck his head through the window, hoping to understand everything the man said.

". . . The kid told us he wasn't alone . . . no, I can't be sure . . . yeah, well, he said they had pictures . . . that's right, pictures . . ."

Scott whirled to face Ellie. "Jimbo's told them we were with him."

"They'll look for us."

"No—they won't think we're on the truck. But they'll guess whoever took the pictures'll call the police."

". . . Maybe he's lying, I don't know, but if he's not . . . yeah, well, I thought you ought to know . . . you do that—you take care of things at that end . . . but, Dave, what'll we do with the kid?"

Scott strained as hard as he could, attempting to hear every word.

"Hey, that's a good idea . . . we'll just hand him over to the people in Columbus."

When the truck was moving once more, Scott turned again to Ellie. "I wish he'd stop at a service station."

"That's where we were."

"Yeah, but nobody could get out safely. We weren't ready."

Ellie was silent for a while, then she touched his arm. "I was thinking, Scott—maybe you're right. Maybe you'd better stay here and try to help Jimbo."

"And you'll climb out?"

"Yes. I'm pretty quick. And"—she pointed down to her jeans and shirt—"everything I'm wearing is dark.

37

If you can make them stop, I'll climb over the side."

"Good, good. But are you sure you aren't afraid?"

"Oh, I'm scared. I'm really scared. But if we don't do it, what'll they do to us when they find us in—wherever they're going?"

Scott nodded. "I'm scared, too," he admitted, "but we can't just sit here and get caught like Jimbo."

Feeling the back of his small camera, he undid the tiny latch and very carefully removed the film cartridge. He took the small box from his pocket and slipped the film into it. "Here, put it where you won't lose it."

Ellie took the little parcel, carefully tied it inside a handkerchief, and rammed it deep into her jeans. "Got it," she said.

As soon as the truck was moving cleanly down the highway, Scott eased open the Mercedes's door and felt his way to the truck bed. Ellie followed him, and they worked their way to the rear of the vehicle. Scott touched her shoulder and pointed to the right side of the bed. "There," he whispered. "You can slip past that stack of little parts-boxes and get to the stake side. The tarp's loose at the corner. You get ready, but don't try climbing over until I give you a signal."

"I'm scared," Ellie said again, "but all right. I'll do it. You say when."

Scott carefully felt among the parts for one he could pick up and shove over the rear gate—something not too heavy for him to lift but big enough to make a loud clatter. After feeling several, he found a hood with a fancy ornament at the front end. He tested its heft, discovered that without too much effort he could move it to the rear gate, and cautiously tugged it from the stack. He had to take his time, though, because he didn't want the ornament to get caught in the tarp. After several minutes, he had it close enough to lift it over. He braced himself, gently pushed the tarp to the side, took a deep breath, and heaved it out.

He had expected it to crash with a loud bang when it hit the pavement, but he had not expected the sparks. It startled him, and he dropped the tarp's edge abruptly.

Almost at once, he felt the vehicle being braked and heard the tires squealing. As soon as the truck stopped, he ducked behind a box filled with engine parts.

The driver's door opened and Charlie climbed out. "*What* was that?"

"Sounded like a fender fell off," came Jake's voice from inside the truck cab.

Scott could not see until Charlie walked past the truck's rear, but the headlights of a passing automobile showed the man trotting in the direction of the hood. Scott glanced quickly around and made out the shadow of Ellie, standing near the side of the stake body. "Wait," he whispered.

Charlie came back, holding the hood halfway over his head. He was cursing with every step. "I told you and Hunker to tie these things down," he called out to Jake. Without waiting for a response, he grunted and lifted until he had the hood over the side and once more onto the truck bed. Before returning to the cab, he pulled the tarp tight at the corner and tied its holding rope.

Scott counted three, and then turned toward Ellie. "Now!" His hissing whisper sounded like a tire losing air.

She hesitated only long enough to nod. Then she slipped up the edge of the tarp, caught the top rail, and almost vaulted over the side. Scott heard only a soft thud as she touched the ground.

"Hey," Jake said, his voice rumbling through the night air. "I heard something."

"Likely a dog," Charlie answered.

Scott wanted to call out "Good luck!" but he dared not raise his voice.

The truck engine roared once more, the gears made a heavy grinding noise, and the vehicle lurched forward. Scott caught at the tarp and raised it, hoping to get a final glimpse of Ellie. All he saw, however, was the side of the road, ending in the dark shadows at a woodland's edge.

Chapter Four

Though it seemed longer, it was only twenty minutes after Walter Parks had used the Herron telephone to call him that Sheriff Timothy Blake joined the families where the bicycles had been located. He introduced himself and nodded toward the deputy who'd accompanied him. "Jason Ling," he said.

"Thanks for coming," Ralph Hamner said. Then he explained how the young people had left home for an afternoon of taking pictures. "It's not like them to stay out after dark."

"How old are they?"

"Scott's thirteen," Alice said.

Louise gave Jimbo's and Ellie's ages. "They're not all that little, Sheriff, but I don't think Jimbo's ever been in this area before."

The sheriff walked across the street and stared out into

41

the pine field. "Easy to get lost, but the field's not that big, either." He turned back. "Tell you what—Ling, you stay here with the bicycles. I'll drive with these people out to the highway and cut through the Ferguson farm road. Could be they're on the other side and can't see how to get through the woods."

They had to backtrack through the several subdivisions that comprised the area known as Mountain Heights; then they headed south once more along Highway 71. A mile past the Mountain Heights Shopping Plaza, the sheriff slowed down and made a left turn. Easing off the highway, he stopped the cruiser with the headlights illuminating a wide fence with a POSTED sign attached to it. "Old man Jeb Ferguson had quite a farm till those sinkholes began appearing," he said. "Had to give it up because they suspected that an old mine beneath the land was caving in."

"I remember," Ralph Hamner said. "That was about ten years ago, wasn't it?"

"Something like that."

"And how far is it to the river?"

"Here at the fence, it's about half a mile. Down at the old home place it's maybe three hundred, four hundred yards." He climbed out of the cruiser and checked the latch on the gate. Fortunately, there was no chain and the gate swung easily. He drove in and moved slowly along the rutted path.

"Looks like it's been used recently," Ralph said.

"It does, at that," the sheriff said. He drove several

hundred yards, slowed at a particularly deep rut, then at a sharp turn he pulled off to the left. "I think we're just about opposite the place where the bicycles are."

Louise turned and looked to her left. "And that field of trees stretches all the way to where we were?"

"It does. And that's why I think maybe your kids could get lost. Likely didn't stop to think about directions. And one part of a pine forest looks like any other." Sheriff Blake climbed out and swept the immediate area with his flashlight. "Do you have lights?"

"I do," Ralph said.

"Good, good. Mr. Parks, Mr. Hamner, you two walk back about fifty yards, then turn toward the river. If they're around here and see the light, you'll hear from them. But watch for those sinkholes—I understand some of them are pretty deep."

"What about us?" Louise asked.

"You can come with me," the sheriff said. "Walking's easier, and we can work along the edge of the pine field. Frankly, though, I don't expect them to be around here. My guess is that they've wandered toward the east—it's easier walking."

As they all climbed out of the cruiser, Walter stopped long enough to help Alice step over a clump of weeds. "Tell me, Sheriff, does that Ferguson fellow still live here?"

"Nope. Moved out about four, five years back. Left his son in charge of the place. Dave Ferguson runs a small trucking firm out the highway a couple or three miles."

"Dave Ferguson, Dave Ferguson," Ralph repeated. "That name rings a bell. I'm a lawyer, Sheriff—was he in some kind of trouble recently? Income taxes or something?"

"I wouldn't be surprised about the taxes bit, but I think you're referring to the overweight trucks—yes, he did have some difficulty. . . ."

Dave Ferguson pulled his automobile into one of the company's parking slots and slammed the brakes. He jumped out and hurried inside. Grabbing the phone, he rapidly dialed a number, then tapped the desk top until he heard a click. "Hunker—Dave. I want you, Lou, Tommy, and the Lucas brothers to come to the shop. We've got trouble."

As soon as he'd hung up the phone, Dave rushed out of the small, cluttered office and turned on the overhead lights in his garage. The front wheels were off one of his stake-bed trucks, the hood was raised on the small van, and two of his movers were parked in such a manner that it would require a lot of jockeying to get them out. He looked at them all, then trotted over to the enclosed orange truck, the one with DANGER—EXPLOSIVES painted on its side. "It'll have to do," he said to himself.

Fifteen minutes later, he heard three vehicles park in the side lot, one behind the other. He was back inside the office when the five men came traipsing in.

Hunker had a can of beer in his hand. "What's going on that's worth rousting us this time of night?"

"That blame kid," Dave said.

"I thought Charlie and Jake took him with them."

"They did. But they took the tape off his mouth, and he told them he wasn't alone."

"So—"

"So," and Dave hit the desk top with his fist, "whoever was with him took pictures."

Hunker was raising the beer can to his mouth, but he stopped abruptly. "That's a mess—man, do you know what kind of mess that can be?"

"I know, I know," Dave said. "Now here's what I want you to do." His gaze swept all of them. "I want you to get the powder truck over to the barn—get that stuff hauled out. Now. Tonight."

"We can't use the powder truck," Hunker said. "Regulations—"

"*Forget* the regulations," Dave said. "If those pictures get to the wrong people, you know what that can mean."

Hunker lowered the beer can. "It could mean a rap. I mean, a long rap. But what about the kid?"

"I told Charlie to take him to Columbus—"

"He'll talk."

"*Not* while he's in Columbus, he won't." Dave turned to Lou, Tommy, and Jamie and Will Lucas. "I want you four to load everything—I mean *everything* in sight."

"Boss," the shortest of the five said. "What about the cars?"

"You're the mechanic, Tommy—how many'll run?"

"Most'll run a little."

45

"Okay. As soon as the barn's clear, run 'em in the river. Hunker, you drive the powder truck off the farm and head south."

"To where?"

"*I don't care where!* Take any back road you come to."

"Are you coming to the farm with us?"

"I'll follow you in the pickup. But I want to call Columbus first. They've got a right to know about the kid coming."

Three minutes later, all five of the men were in the explosive hauler and on their way. Dave watched out the side window until they had disappeared, then he sat at the battered desk chair and picked up the phone. He dialed a number, waited until it had rung twice, hung up, and repeated the process two more times. Only then did he let it ring until somebody answered. "Jeffrey, Dave here . . . yeah, Dave Ferguson . . . that's right . . . yeah, it's on the way. Should get there around midnight or shortly after, but I've got a problem . . . I'm sending you a smart-aleck kid," and briefly, he explained the story. "I don't care what you do with him . . . just keep him hidden and out of sight for a week or so. . . . No, nothing like that, you're holding him . . . yeah, for a friend. . . ."

Chapter Five

Ellie found that walking along the gravel highway shoulder was not as easy as it might have seemed. It was one thing to walk through the field of trees and along that dusty farm path in soft-soled shoes, but here the chunks of gravel and bigger rocks dug into the bottoms of her feet.

She wished she had a flashlight so she could see the surface of this untraveled road. As it was, she never knew whether it would be smooth and even or rutted and grooved. When she tried to anticipate one step, thinking it would be like the one before, she misjudged and almost tripped. When she tried to feel her way by sliding her foot along, she found herself almost falling forward. She finally decided that the best procedure was to move farther from the pavement, even if it meant walking in the drainage ditch.

Scott had said he was going to help Jimbo; but Ellie couldn't decide whether that was to keep her from being hurt or to make it easier for himself, once the truck reached that place—what was it?—Columbus. She wished they'd just gone on across the field to the river. They could have taken all the pictures Scott might have wanted, they could have gone home in plenty of time for her to see that TV special she'd been planning to watch. And right about now they'd be—wait a minute—what would they be doing? Eating? But no, it was past dinnertime. Maybe they'd be watching TV? Or getting ready for bed?

She wished she'd worn her watch.

After walking for what seemed like half an hour, she paused at a gentle turn in the road and looked in every direction. Nothing, not even one glowing light to mark the place of a house or store. If there'd been houses along the way, their lights must have been out. She certainly hadn't seen anything.

She stood still long enough to catch her breath, then started forward.

Something in the brush stirred, and she stopped suddenly.

There it was again.

An animal—it had to be an animal. Nobody would be hiding in the bushes along this forsaken stretch of highway. It had to be a dog or cat. Somebody'd come along and dumped a pet. She thought that was the cruelest thing people could do—dump a tamed animal in the woods and leave it to fend for itself.

The bushes moved once more. Ellie stopped. "Here—here, boy—that's a good dog, come on."

The bushes gave no sound.

"Come on, kitty, good kitty, that's a good kitty, come on."

But the sudden sound was that of neither a puppy nor a cat. It was soft, somewhere between the bleat of a lamb and the whimper of a dog. And although Ellie could not see through the dark shadows, she knew that the creature posed no threat. The tension left her, and she started again.

She took five steps and hesitated. She took three more and stopped. She had to hurry. She had to get to a telephone and call her aunt, let her and Uncle Walter know where she was and what had happened to Jimbo and Scott. She had to get the film to someone who could develop it.

But the little creature in the brush—she couldn't just walk away and leave it.

She turned about and retraced her steps to the source of the sound. She moved across the drainage ditch and climbed the shallow bank. Near the heavy bush, she bent low and made a clicking sound with her tongue.

Again, the little whimper responded.

She pushed the tall weeds aside. And just as the moon came out from behind the clouds, she looked down. A

49

tiny fawn was lying on its side, its head up and its ears forward. Enough of the bright moonlight fell on it for Ellie to see that one of its hind legs was drawn up and bleeding. "Oh, oh," she said softly.

The animal turned its head and seemed to struggle.

Ellie bent down and cautiously put her hand on the small body. Instantly, the fawn tried to raise itself. It got its head and shoulders up on wobby front legs, but it could not raise its hind quarters.

Gently, Ellie touched its neck, ran her fingers along its side. "Poor little thing," she said. "Did an old car hit you?" She patted its side, then rubbed her hand over its head. Beneath the soft skin, she felt the quick trembling, the little heart racing. "I won't hurt you, little thing," she said. "I won't hurt you."

The fawn tried once more to stand. It could not.

Ellie knew she had to hurry. Scott was depending on her to telephone for help.

But she didn't think she could hurry—not while her thoughts were on a little deer, lying in the bushes all by itself.

She bent lower, put one hand beneath the small body, and very carefully lifted it. The fawn kicked its forefeet and wiggled its frail body. Ellie stood, then tenderly cradled the animal in one arm, as if she were carrying a baby. "Don't worry," she said. "I won't leave you here by yourself."

She eased down the shallow bank to the road's edge. She paused for a brief moment, then set off walking

50

again. And as she moved on, she realized that for a reason she could not explain she was not as frightened as she had been only minutes earlier.

She had walked at least half a mile from where she'd found the fawn before she saw any kind of light. Then, off to her left, she spotted a house.

Had to be a house. Not enough lights for it to be a store, and it was back from the road. The sight made her walk faster, and within half a minute she came to a winding dirt driveway. She paused a moment, then turned and followed it.

When she made the last little turn and came to a small clearing, she discovered that the house was actually a small mobile home, half-hidden by the surrounding growth of tall pines and oaks. The source of the light that had guided her was nothing more than a naked bulb jutting out over a small door.

Ellie looked at it for a moment, all the while gently patting the fawn. Then she stepped briskly forward and rapped on the metal side of the home.

No one responded. But she heard a radio going and guessed that she had not knocked loudly enough. She shifted the fawn to her left arm and this time knocked as hard as she could.

"Yeah?" The voice frightened her. "Who's that?"

Ellie swallowed hard. "I—I need help," she called out.

"Go away. We got no help to give."

She knocked once more.

"I said go away—git!"

Ellie didn't like the sound of his voice, but she had no intention of going away. She needed to use a phone and had to make the people inside realize that. Taking a deep breath, she set her fist and knocked a third time.

At once, she heard heavy feet on the thin floor. The inside door swung suddenly open, and a man bare to the waist and holding a can of beer in his hand peered out. "Hey, didn't you hear me—we don't want no comp'ny."

Any other time, Ellie would have turned and run off. She thought the man's beard was the ugliest one she'd ever seen. His hair was a tangled mop, and she guessed by the tone of his voice that the beer he was holding wasn't his first of the evening. "I'm not company, mister—but I'm lost and I need to use a telephone."

The man peered down at her, bent forward further, and stared at the fawn. "Holy catfish," he said, then laughed. "Hon! Hey, Hon—c'm 'ere an' see who we got come callin'!"

Moments later a barefooted young woman in a loose shirt and faded cut-offs joined the man. Like him, she was holding a can of beer. "Lordy, lordy, no tellin' what'll come crawlin' outa them woods."

Ellie stared from one to the other. "May I use your telephone?" she said. Inside, she felt tension and anger, but she tried to keep her voice from betraying her feelings. "I have to call the police."

"Whooo, whooo," the man said, "now, ain't that somethin'. Here we got a little tramp demandin' to use the phone, saying' she needs the law. Y' know, Hon, ain't no tellin' what people'll think of next—sendin' a kid to call the law."

Ellie matched him stare for stare. "Mister, do you have a telephone I can use?"

"Hey, kid, who's to call anybody from out here?" The woman took a swallow from her can. "But I tell you what." She nudged the man. "You c'n come on in an' join the party." She laughed. "How 'bout it, Eddie, can't she come join th' party?"

The man laughed with her and pushed the screen back. "Yeah—and bring ya little kitty—hey, that ain't no kitty-cat, that there's a baby deer. Yeah—bring the animal, too—make a real party. Ain't nothin' good as fresh young deer meat." He bent low and suddenly reached out, as if to take the fawn from Ellie.

She jerked away, almost stumbling. "Don't touch him!" She took another step backward. "Can I use your telephone or not?"

The woman laughed. "Kid, didn't he tell you? Ain't no telephone in this part of the county—ain't enough houses for lines to be run. Ain't likely you'll find one less'n five miles west of here."

Ellie turned toward the man. "You don't have one?"

"Don't nobody in these parts have one, so why don't you just f'rgit the phone. Come on in an' join the party."

Ellie shook all over in spite of herself. Five miles, the woman had said. Five miles. She didn't think she could walk that far. She and the boys had walked two, maybe

53

three, miles taking all those pictures. She had been cramped up in that Mercedes for at least an hour. And she guessed she'd walked at least three miles since climbing off the truck.

She turned around and headed back down the driveway.

"Hey, kid, don't leave mad!"

She kept walking until she reached the curve. And at that point anger and exhaustion made her stop and look back. "Mister, I don't want anything to do with you!"

Without waiting for the comment she knew he'd make, she tucked the fawn in the crook of her arm once more and struck out down the gravel drive toward the road.

Chapter Six

Although the ropes binding his wrists and ankles were not tight enough to cut off circulation, Jimbo's arms and legs were beginning to feel numb. And though the blindfold wasn't binding, every time he tried to blink his eyes the rough cloth scratched his eyelids. His stomach felt empty, his throat was dry, and his lips wanted to stick together. "My daddy's sure going to get somebody," he said.

"Look, kid," Charlie said, "ain't nobody going to get nobody. You just keep still, don't say nothing, and won't anybody hurt you."

"Well, I'm hungry and thirsty and my daddy won't like it when he finds out I've been starved."

Jake laughed. "Kid, much as you run that mouth of yours, I'd bet your old man'd be glad to have somebody take you off his hands. Tell you what—soon's we git where we're going, you can call him and tell him how mean we are. Okay?"

"Shut up," Charlie said.

"Now wait a minute—"

"I said, shut up," Charlie repeated. "We got a job to do and that's what we're aiming on. Nothing else. Understand?"

"Yeah—well," Jake said, "it's a dull ride. All I'm doin's tryin' to have a little fun."

"This ain't no fun trip."

"Okay, okay," Jake said. He turned and stared out the window. "Wonder what Dave's up to now?"

Charlie made a sound, taking a deep breath. "Probably trying to get everything out of the barn. He'd better—if the kid's right and somebody took pictures, they better get rid of all the stuff."

"That won't stop the pictures."

"Yeah, but pictures won't convict nobody of nothing," Charlie said. "You got to have hard evidence."

"Well, I hope he gets it out—hope he dumps it in the river," Jake said. He glanced at Jake. "Kid, how come you and your friends had to bust in that way, anyhow?"

"Didn't bust in," Jimbo said. "But if you weren't doing something bad, nobody'd care." He sniffed. "Anyway, I don't think there was any film in the camera." He knew better. He'd held the box while Scott put the cartridge in place. But maybe if he could make them think they had not been photographed, they'd turn him loose.

Charlie didn't buy the idea. "That's the way with most

56

people," he said, mocking Jimbo. "They go around taking pictures without using film."

Jimbo swallowed and tried to lick his lips. His tongue was too dry, however, to give him any relief.

Dave Ferguson gave Hunker and the others five minutes, then he closed the office, leaving only one small light burning, and hurried out to the pickup. He meant to follow them—to make sure they got all the parts loaded and that every one of the cars in the small lot got moved.

He made the five-mile drive in a little over five minutes, slowed as he neared the dirt road turnoff, and carefully maneuvered through the narrow opening in the fence. The gate had been pushed back, and he reminded himself to tell Hunker to close it next time. Shifting to second gear, he eased over the shallow bump and began winding his way toward the barn and old home-place. He'd hardly driven fifty feet, however, when he caught sight of the bobbing light at the edge of the pine field.

Dave drove another hundred yards, made a hard right turn, swung back to the left, and stopped abruptly. There, blocking the road, was his big truck. Standing beside the door was a man with a flashlight. The moment Dave stopped, the light was aimed on his pickup, and as soon as he stepped out, the light was aimed on him. He shaded his eyes and started toward the light. "Hey— what're you people doing on my land?"

The man stepped forward. "Are you Dave Ferguson?"

"I am. Who're you?"

"Sheriff Blake."

Dave quickly changed the tone of his voice. "Oh, Sheriff, sorry. Didn't recognize you. What's the trouble?"

"Is this your truck?"

"It is."

"Do you usually run at night?"

Dave tried to laugh. "Not really running, Sheriff, but a couple of my other trucks are broke down. I sent my men out to get some old parts Dad left in the barn." He shook his head. "Likely they won't help us, but it's too late to get anything from the shops, and we've got some early runs to make."

"But this is a powder truck."

"I know. Dad had half a dozen cases of dynamite—he meant to use them on the sinkholes, but never got around to it. I thought as long as the men were coming out, I'd have them bring the stuff to the warehouse. And you know how the trucking regulations are—you can't haul explosives in anything but an explosive truck."

The sheriff nodded, then turned to the truck. "Okay, go ahead."

"Sheriff," Dave said, "what're you doing out here?"

"Looking for lost kids," and the sheriff told him about Jimbo, Scott, and Ellie. "By the way, you must have been out here today—probably checking on the parts."

"I came out this morning—yes," Dave said. So, he thought quickly, that kid had been right. There'd been

58

three. And if the sheriff was searching the woods and field, that meant whoever took the pictures hadn't gotten to anyone with them. It also meant that the other two were—now wait, wait a minute. If they had not gone home right away—and he doubted they'd have stayed at the barn after the truck left—maybe, just maybe, they'd somehow slipped on the truck and were right now hidden passengers with Charlie and Jake. "I didn't see any children, though." He waved his hand toward the overgrown field. "Most people know enough not to walk around the area—the word's been pretty well spread about the sinkholes here."

Sheriff Blake nodded. "About those holes—are they still posted?"

"The whole farm's posted."

"Kids don't always heed those signs, though."

"Tell you what," Dave said quickly, "I'll have my men make a thorough search around the house and barn before we pick up the parts. It's not likely they're there, but we'll look." He smiled. "If we see anything, I'll come let you know."

"Do that," the sheriff said.

Dave nodded and returned to his truck.

Five minutes later, he joined his men at the barn. "Hunker, you and Lou get busy and load the parts. All of 'em, hear? And Tommy, you and the rest get to those cars in the lot. I want all of 'em in the river!"

Fifteen minutes later, all but three of the cars had been dispatched. Most of the parts had been loaded, and

Dave knew they'd have time. He was beginning to feel relieved—even if the sheriff and those others came this far, they'd find nothing. All he had to do was contact his people in Columbus, tell them to look carefully—there might be two other kids riding in the back of the stake-bed truck.

"Hey, Dave."

He turned from the barn toward the lot. "Yeah, Tommy?"

"The Lincoln's not running and the Chevy battery won't turn the starter."

"Well, push 'em!"

"Man, you've got to be crazy—no way we can push 'em to the river. That's near a quarter-mile."

"If we leave 'em here, the sheriff's going to find them. And Timothy Blake's no dummy." Dave looked around quickly. "Gas—is there any gas here?"

Tommy stared at him. "You mean to burn the cars?"

"I mean to burn the cars and the barn," Dave said. "If one of those kids got pictures and the pictures happen by chance to get into the wrong hands, I don't want anything left that'll be tied to us." He stared hard at Tommy. "You'll stay behind and do it—for a hundred bucks."

"That I'll do," Tommy said.

"Okay. But don't do anything until the truck's gone and I'm on the road. Fill four bottles with gasoline. Wait twenty or thirty minutes—give us plenty of time to be on the highway. Put a match to the barn, then throw the bottles one by one—make it sound like explosions."

"Any reason for that?"

"I told the sheriff we were picking up dynamite. He'll hear and figure that's what's going off."

On the way out of the field, Dave sent the big vehicle on while he stopped for a word with the sheriff. "I didn't see a sign of anybody," he said, leaning out of the pickup's window.

Sheriff Blake nodded. "I appreciate your checking, anyway."

Dave started to drive away, then suddenly pointed across the field. "Did you happen to check the river road?"

"River road?"

"Yeah. Just inside the fence, there's an old truck path—goes to a place we used to call Crooked Leg Bluff. Good place to picnic and watch the river. Dad used to drive there because the fishing's good." He smiled. "Kids like it—at least, they used to."

"I didn't know about it," the sheriff said. "We'll check it out."

"Do that. Good luck—hope you find them soon." Dave drove away, knowing he'd be well off the farm when Tommy set the fire.

An hour later, with the workmen gone and nobody to hear, Dave called Columbus once more. He again asked for Jeffrey. "Look, I told you about the kid they're bringing. Well, it's worse than I thought—there were two others, and they may have slipped on the truck . . . I know it's none of your business. . . . Okay, I realize it's my problem . . . all I want you to do is make sure that if they're on the truck, you keep them there—yeah, yeah, well, stay out of it, then . . . just have Charlie call me as soon as he gets there."

Dave hung up the phone and slapped the desk. "Nobody ever wants to get involved," he muttered. He lighted a cigarette, blew a cloud of smoke, and thoughtfully leaned back in the worn chair.

Chapter Seven

Ellie knew that she ought to hurry, but there was little hurry left in her. She had walked, she had trotted, she had run uncertainly, and she had gone back to walking because her legs were too wobbly to do anything else.

The young fawn had stirred at first, soon after Ellie had left the mobile home. But now it was quiet, its small head resting gently against her chest, and its body was so still that she couldn't help wondering if it had died. She wished she could pause long enough to put it down and drop to the ground beside it. But she knew she could not. Before too long, Jimbo and Scott would be in that place—she thought it was called Columbus—and if she didn't get help soon—well, she didn't want to think what might happen to them if she didn't.

A fleeting cloud passed overhead, and for a moment,

the moon was completely hidden. The road was so dark, she had to stop, fearing that she might trip over an unseen rock. When the cloud moved on, she glanced down at the little fawn. And for the first time since she'd picked it up, she realized it was spotted. Then she remembered—all fawns were spotted until they lost what she supposed was their baby hair. She gently touched its side, let her finger caress its nose, then instinctively held it up to brush her cheek against its soft body. "Little thing," she said, "I won't let you get hurt again."

To help pass the time, she began counting her steps. She told herself that she'd see a light off the road somewhere by the time she reached five hundred.

She did not.

She told herself she'd see one by the time she reached two thousand. She did not.

She'd counted to six thousand and was tired of numbers when she came to a sharp bend in the highway. And there, off to her right and on the other side of the road, she made out a well-lighted house, nestled in the trees but not at all hidden by them. And when she came to the driveway, she wanted to laugh out loud, it was so wide and clear. She could tell that it was freshly paved, and it was almost wide enough for two cars to drive parallel to each other. The people would be nice—that much she was sure of. And best of all, they'd have a telephone.

As tired as she was, Ellie ran the rest of the way to the spacious, columned front porch. Gently cradling the fawn, she mounted the four steps and did not stop until her hand was on the huge brass knocker. She banged it three times, waited a moment, then banged it three times more.

Within moments, she heard muffled footsteps coming toward the door, either house shoes or bare feet—or maybe the floor was carpeted.

A small door within the big one opened abruptly, and a gray-haired woman peered out at her. "Yes—child, who're you?"

Ellie swallowed and forced herself to answer. She gave her name quickly. "I—I need to use a telephone."

"Your folks about?" And the woman stared past her, as if expecting to see an automobile in the drive.

"No, ma'am. I'm by myself. Please, lady, can I use your telephone?"

The woman looked down at the fawn in Ellie's hand. "You got a dog?"

"No, ma'am, it's a baby deer."

"A baby deer?"

"Yes, ma'am—it's been hurt."

"Poor thing. Likely a car hit it."

Ellie cocked her head to one side. "Yes, ma'am. But please, lady, can I use your telephone?"

The woman made no move to unlock the door. "Are you right sure your folks aren't off there by the road?"

Ellie vigorously shook her head. "I'm all by myself, and please, lady, I'm in trouble."

"I reckon you are, child, if you're on the road alone. What kind of trouble you got?"

Ellie swallowed once more. "Ma'am, some men kidnapped me—"

"*Kidnapped?*" The woman closed the security door halfway. "I don't want to get mixed up in anybody's trouble—"

"They're gone," Ellie said. "I escaped, but I need to call my family in Bremerton." She meant Jimbo's family, but there was no time to explain.

"And they're not hunting you?" The woman looked once more past Ellie, as if she might expect to see someone peering at her from the surrounding woods.

"They don't even know I got away," Ellie said. "*Please*, lady—"

"Child, I've got no telephone."

Ellie's shoulders drooped. She took a deep breath. Her shaking hand held the fawn close. "I—I mean, can you tell me how far it is to one?"

"I guess the closest one's at Jarmon's Grocery—about five miles from here."

Ellie shook all over, and she couldn't stop the tear that formed in the corner of her eye. She sniffed, looked down, and gently petted the fawn's tiny head. She started to turn away.

"Only thing we got's a CB radio."

Ellie looked up suddenly. "Can—can you talk as far as to Bremerton with it?"

The woman shook her head slowly. "Best we can do is

maybe fifteen, twenty miles. I reckon it's mighty near fifty from here to Bremerton."

Ellie had read about how CB radios were used in emergencies, and she knew that people talked on them day and night. "Maybe you could talk to somebody and they'd call for me."

"Child, about the only people I can raise on it t'night is a deputy, down at the sheriff's office."

"Does he have a phone?"

"He's got a phone, all right."

"Maybe he'd call somebody for me."

The woman hesitated a moment longer, then turned halfway around. "Jerry, can you come to the door?"

Ellie touched the fawn's body, gently rubbing its back. But her eyes were on the small opening where the woman stood. She heard shuffling feet—bare ones, this time she was sure about it. A balding, round-faced man appeared beside the woman. His heavy glasses, shadowed as they were, seemed unusually dark. "Yeah?"

"There's a child on the porch, says she's been kidnapped and got away."

The man shook his head, but Ellie could tell he wasn't looking at her. "Folks'll say anything," he said, his voice deep and soft. "Can't be too careful."

"She wants to know can we call the sheriff on the CB."

"Reckon we can. But for what?"

"To get him to use his telephone—call her folks in Bremerton."

"Bremerton? That's a piece from here. Child,"—as he

tried to fix his stare in her direction but actually looked to the side, Ellie realized that he was blind—"are you sure you're telling the truth?"

"Yes, sir. We were playing near an old barn and some men took Jimbo—that's my cousin—and I climbed on the truck with Scott because we thought we could help—"

"Wait, wait, child. Hold on, not so fast. You want me to holler at the sheriff's deputy, ask him to call somebody in Bremerton, for him to say you're here. Right?"

"Yes, sir. My name's Ellie Whittington, but if he can call the residence of Walter Parks—"

"Who's Walter Parks?"

"He's my uncle," Ellie said, "and I'm visiting his family."

The man cocked his head to one side, seemed to look off into space a moment. "Martha, you stay here with the child—I'll make the call."

Ellie wanted to go inside, she wanted to be right there when the sheriff or one of his deputies answered. Yet she knew the woman meant for her to remain where she was. The man disappeared, and Ellie glanced down at the fawn.

"How'd you come to catch the animal?" The woman's voice seemed to be softer now.

"It was lying beside the road—I think maybe a car hit it."

"Poor little thing. Likely it'll die."

"If I can get some water to wash its hurt and maybe put on a bandage, it won't."

The woman seemed to smile, but she made no move to unlock the main door. "Time'll tell. Now, you just wait there. Jerry'll be back directly."

Ellie waited for what seemed like ten minutes, then she heard the steps crossing the floor and the man appeared once more beside the woman. "Deputy Sims called the place you said. Nobody answered."

Ellie felt a sudden tightness building up inside her. Someone had to be home, just had to be home. Where would they go? Where'd they be, if they weren't at home? She took a deep breath. "Maybe they're next door—that's where Scott lives. Can you ask him to call the residence of Mr. Hamner—Mr. Ralph Hamner?"

"Mr. Ralph Hamner," the man repeated. "I'll ask."

Again, he turned and disappeared. Again, he was gone for several minutes. And when he returned this time, he was shaking his head. "Don't anybody answer there, either."

Ellie sighed and bowed her head and closed her eyes. "Lady, mister, I'm scared . . . real scared."

Barely twenty minutes after Dave Ferguson had driven away, the searchers were in the sheriff's patrol car, slowly making their way toward Crooked Leg Bluff. "Hasn't been driven over in a while," the sheriff said. He was braking for a rut when Ralph turned around.

"Sheriff! Over there!"

The sheriff stopped the car and whirled about in the seat. The sudden flames sprang upward, searing the night as they climbed angrily into the blackness. "The old barn—"

But before he could finish the sentence, the night air was blasted into turmoil by one explosion, then another, then a third and fourth. "Good Lord!" The sheriff accelerated suddenly, spun the cruiser about, and raced back toward the main farm road, at the same time grabbing the mike to his police radio. He called headquarters and reported the fire. "Better have Chief Hollister send a pumper," he said.

He retraced his route, cut a hard right at the main road Dave had taken earlier, and proceeded to the older fence that surrounded the homestead area. There, they all climbed out and stared at the crackling flames.

Alice shielded her face from the heat. "Maybe," she said, "if the kids are in the woods, they'll see the fire and work their way toward it."

"Let's hope so," Ralph said.

Within minutes, the rising and falling wail of a firetruck siren broke through the noise, and all of them turned to watch as the big vehicle came bouncing over the narrow, rutted farm road. Its powerful headlights cut wide swaths in the darkness as it rumbled toward the old barn, and its smaller, revolving lights made an eerie, uneven pattern in the night. Walter and Ralph pulled

Louise and Alice out of the road and into the weeds just before the truck roared past them.

As the vehicle moved toward the worst of the fire, Sheriff Blake gave his head a little shake. "Strange," he said, as if talking to himself. "Mighty strange. I wonder what set it off."

Chapter Eight

Ellie stood there on the porch, first staring at the two people inside the safety of their home, then glancing down at the gentle fawn. She took a deep breath, sighed, and slowly turned around. She did not want to cry. She did not want to let them know how very frightened and alone she felt. The woman had said there was a telephone at some store called Jarmon's. She'd just have to draw herself up and walk to it.

But she was hungry. And she was very thirsty. She'd have to sit for a while and catch her breath.

She moved to the edge of the porch, glanced at the steps, then turned to look back at the house. The couple still watched. "Ma'am, if you don't mind, I'd sure like to sit on your steps a little while."

For the first time since she'd arrived, she detected a

softer quality in the woman's voice as she said, "Sit, child. And if you'd like it, I'll bring you a glass of water."

"I'd like it fine. Thank you."

She was still at the edge of the porch when the woman returned and opened the door. "Sorry about your trouble, child," she said. She nodded toward the door. "Sorry, too, we have to be so cautious, but a body never knows who's coming to knock you in the head."

"Yes, ma'am," Ellie said. She lifted the glass and drank slowly. When she'd downed half of its contents, she lowered it. "I guess I'd be scared, too, if I lived way off here, with nobody else nearby—"

"Martha!" The man's voice carried out to the porch. "That little girl—is she gone?"

The woman turned around. "She's drinking some water!"

"Well, tell her to wait."

Ellie looked quizzically at the woman. But before either had a chance to speak, the man joined his wife. "It's the deputy on the CB—says can she talk to him."

The woman looked from him to Ellie. "Well—well, I see no reason why she can't."

Ellie looked down at the fawn, then faced the woman. "I can't just turn it loose."

"Of course you can't," the woman said. "You wait right here—I'll fetch a box."

Moments later, after gently placing the little animal in the box the woman brought her, Ellie found herself in

73

a well-furnished room with cabinets full of records and a very unusual record player on a stand near the window. Across from it, on a well-equipped table, was the largest citizens band radio she'd ever seen. The man held out a mike and waited until she'd taken it from him. "Did you ever talk on one of these?"

"A few times. Back home my next-door neighbor had a CB in his car."

"Then you know how to call on it." The man moved aside. "The deputy goes by the handle of 'Bird Dog'— just call him."

Ellie fingered the small key on the mike's side. She squeezed it gently and held the instrument to her mouth. "Hello—Mr. Bird Dog, it's me—Ellie Whittington."

At once the static cleared. "Ellie, this is Bird Dog— Deputy Long of the Durango County Sheriff's Department. I've just talked to Deputy Harris, Bremerton County, and he tells me the sheriff's with a search party. Do you know anything about it?"

Ellie was puzzled. "No, sir." She hesitated a moment. "Who are they searching for?"

"He didn't give me any names, but he said they were looking for three children."

Ellie shivered all over. Three—Jimbo, Scott, and me. "I—I was with two other friends. Jimbo Parks and Scott Hamner." She cleared her throat. "We were out taking pictures of trees and things in the woods and we went to an old barn and some men grabbed Jimbo—" She caught

74

herself, suddenly wondering if she should say anything else. She released the key.

"Okay, Ellie—just hold on a minute. I've got Deputy Harris on the phone. Let me see what he can tell me."

Ellie turned and looked at the man. He had moved from the desk and was now standing beside a large brown recliner, one hand on its back. He was facing her almost as if he could see her, and she saw a kindness in his face that had not been evident earlier.

The static on the CB growled, then abruptly cleared. "Ellie, what were the names of your friends?"

"Jimbo and Scott—Jimbo Parks and Scott Hamner."

"Ten-four. Stand by."

Ellie looked about. The man was almost smiling. "Did you know what that meant?" he asked.

"Ten-four? No, sir, I'm not sure."

"Means, okay. Means, I heard you clearly."

The deputy's voice came once more, and this time there was an air of urgency in its tone. "Big Look, Bird Dog here. She's telling the truth. Sheriff Blake and his people are searching for her and her friends."

The man took the mike from Ellie. "Ten-four, Bird Dog. And she was really kidnapped?"

"She got there somehow," the deputy said. "I'll be with you in about ten minutes."

"You're coming here for her?"

"I am," the deputy said. "This thing may be a lot bigger than just three lost children."

It was bigger, Ellie thought. And the knowledge that

she'd at last contacted somebody who cared made her—well, she just couldn't help it, she gave a little cry and tears welled up in her eyes.

The woman smiled softly and crossed the room toward her. "Child, I'm sorry—so sorry we didn't do something for you sooner. But we didn't know."

"I understand," Ellie said.

The deputy had said ten minutes, but Ellie didn't think it was that long when they heard the screech of tires on the highway and the roar of a speeding vehicle as it turned onto the wide drive. Ellie and the woman went to the door as Deputy Long ran up onto the porch. He stopped abruptly when he spotted the fawn. "*Where* did that come from?"

Ellie glanced down at the animal and realized she was smiling. "I found it," she said, and explained how she'd been carrying it as she walked along the highway.

The man bent down and looked at the fawn a moment. "I don't think it's hurt too bad," he said. "A little disinfectant and some bandaging, and it'll be good as new." He rose and turned to Ellie, smiling. "The Bremerton sheriff's office is getting word to the families," he said. "Meantime, I'm taking you back to our office." The smile faded. "Were you hurt?"

"No, sir. The men didn't even see me and Scott."

"You can tell me what happened on the way." He turned to the woman. "Tell Big Look I'll catch him on the two-way and fill him in on the details. Right now, Ellie and I have to move."

76

The woman nodded, then turned to Ellie. "Child! I forgot my manners. I bet you're hungry."

"I guess so," Ellie said. "But I didn't think about it."

"I'll just rustle up something—"

"We can't take time," Deputy Long said. "If the boys are being held, we've got to get help—"

"Pshaw," the woman broke in. "I'll cut her some cake—she can eat that on the way."

As they sped in the patrol car back to the deputy's office, Ellie was finishing the large slice of cake and letting the fawn lick her fingers while she gave Deputy Long the details of their experience. "We didn't really mean to go," she said. "We were just trying to get Jimbo away from them," and she gave him the facts about the truck, about the men, and about hiding inside the Mercedes.

"How'd you escape?"

"It was Scott's idea," she said, then explained about the hood being thrown off. "I don't think they had any idea how it fell."

"That was clever thinking," the deputy said. "But what about the pictures—didn't you say this Scott took some?"

"He did." She reached inside her jeans pocket and brought out the cartridge. "I don't know if they're any good. He couldn't use the flash, and it was sort of dark in the barn."

Minutes later, they pulled into the parking area beside a small brick building. "Come on inside," Deputy

Long said. "We'll call Sheriff Blake's office, then we'll see to the pictures. And," he glanced at the little fawn, "your friend."

Ellie climbed out, being careful not to let the door bump the animal, and followed the deputy inside. He pointed to an empty carton in the corner. "Put it there," he said, "and I'll get some first-aid stuff you can use while I call."

While she waited, Ellie dropped to her knees and looked into the small creature's face. "I don't know what your name ought to be, but I think I'll call you Lucky. That's what we both are, I guess. Just lucky."

Sheriff Blake was still standing near the barn, watching the firemen spray the flames, when his walkie-talkie squawked. He keyed the mike. "Blake here."

"Sheriff, Deputy Harris. I've just gotten a phone call from a Deputy Long, Durango County. He's picked up a young girl who says she's Ellie Whittington."

Sheriff Blake cupped his hand over the small speaker. "Say again? Did you say Ellie Whittington?"

"That's the name he gave me."

"Hold it right there." Sheriff Blake whirled about. "Mr. Parks, what was the girl's name again?"

"Ellie," Walter said. "Ellie Whittington. Why?"

Once more, Sheriff Blake pressed the walkie-talkie speaking key. "Harris, give me all the details."

"Deputy Long said he has Ellie Whittington with him," the deputy repeated.

78

"*What!*" Louise broke from Walter's side and bent over the small radio. "*What* did he say?"

"Repeat," the sheriff said. "And tell me everything."

"The girl's with him at his office now," the deputy said. "The two boys are in a truck on their way to Columbus."

"On their way *where*?" Walter said.

The sheriff raised a hand, interrupting him. "Go on."

"She says the men who took them are part of a car theft and chop shop ring—"

"How does she know that?"

"She says they saw some men working in an old barn and that's what the boy named Scott called them." The deputy proceeded to give all the information that had been relayed to him. "The girl's okay, Sheriff, but the two boys are still on the truck, so far as she knows. And on their way to Columbus."

When the sheriff had all the information his deputy could give him, he turned to Walter and Ralph. "You heard—"

"They've been kidnapped," Louise broke in. "Kidnapped!" She choked back a sob and turned to Alice. "We shouldn't have let them leave the house."

"Now, now, Louise," her husband said, taking her arm, "we don't have all the story yet." He turned to the sheriff. "Now what?"

Without answering, the sheriff again pressed the walkie-talkie key. "Harris, what did the Durango deputy say about the pictures?"

"He said Ellie had a film cartridge. He called his photographer and they're going to develop them now."

"Good, good."

"But how can they develop pictures in the sheriff's office?" Louise asked. "And what good'll that do? Somebody has to go find Jimbo and Scott."

"If they took pictures," the sheriff said quietly, "maybe they got one of the truck's tag. Maybe of the people. That film cartridge may be the best thing we have going for us now."

"Why can't somebody just go to wherever the truck was heading and—"

"The girl said they were heading for Columbus," Sheriff Blake interrupted. "And don't worry—we'll be after them." He hesitated, glancing off toward the barn. "Something bothers me, though, about this fire. How did it happen just now? And how is it that just before the fire started, Ferguson and his people went there, hauling material?"

"You don't think he had anything to do—but no," Walter said, interrupting himself, "the man would have been plain stupid, coming here if he'd had anything to do with the kids' disappearance."

"We'll find out." Sheriff Blake once more keyed the walkie-talkie. "Harris, Blake. Get somebody to find Dave Ferguson . . . that's right, Mr. Dave Ferguson, of Ferguson Trucking. I think we need to talk to him about a certain matter." He paused a moment, then added, "Tell me, is the 'copter ready to fly?"

80

Louise turned to her husband. "What's that for?"

"I don't know," he said softly. "Let's see."

"Right, right. Well, call Lovett and tell him to meet me at the airport. And Harris, call Captain Brady— that's Henderson Brady, Civil Air Patrol. Ask him if he can fly a party of—wait, now,"—the sheriff glanced toward Walter and Ralph, got a nod from them—"four to Columbus." He listened a moment longer, then said, "Right. Get back to that Durango deputy. Tell him someone'll be there as soon as the 'copter can make it."

When he'd put the walkie-talkie back in his holster, he turned to the women. "Mrs. Parks, Mrs. Hamner, I'm flying the 'copter to the Durango sheriff's office. If either of you wants to go along—"

"What about Columbus?" Alice asked.

"I'm sending my chief deputy, Alonzo Townsend," the sheriff answered. "And," he glanced at Ralph and Walter, "if you two want to go with them, there'll be room for you."

"We do," Ralph said, and got an agreeing nod from Walter.

"On the trip to Columbus," the sheriff said, "I think it's best if you ladies don't go with them."

"Then," Alice caught Louise's hand, "we'll both go to Durango County with you."

Louise took a deep breath and put her hand on her husband's shoulder. "And please, God, let the boys be all right," she said softly.

Chapter Nine

As the truck sped along the last stretch of highway toward Columbus, Scott realized that he should have a plan to free Jimbo. He knew that whatever he chose to do, it would take time—time that he didn't have unless he created a problem for Charlie and Jake.

He thought about the hood he'd thrown off the back so Ellie could slip over the side. He supposed he could do that once more. He could raise the rear of the tarpaulin as he'd done then, carefully lift the lighter parts, and ease them over the gate. They'd make noise, Charlie would stop and retrieve them, and they'd be that much later arriving in Columbus.

But there was the other possibility. Charlie might wonder how two or three additional parts could simply bounce off, and he might just climb onto the bed to see for himself. With a flashlight, he would most certainly find the reason—and Scott would be tied up as Jimbo was.

Anyway, that wouldn't give extra time when they reached Columbus, and that's what he needed.

As he frantically racked his brain, trying to come up with a workable idea, he let his hand stray from the Mercedes steering wheel to the instrument panel. His fingers touched the radio controls, the cigarette lighter, the gearshift. He slouched down and casually felt beneath the panel, and his fingers found a wire.

Hey, a wire!

He sat up suddenly. He could jerk out wires, he could jam paper into the ignition key slot.

He thought about the idea. Maybe if he disabled the Mercedes and it wouldn't start, if he fixed it so it couldn't roll, even with help Charlie and Jake would have to take extra time unloading it. Somehow, when they arrived at their destination, he intended slipping out and hiding. And while they were working on the automobile, trying to unload it, he could free Jimbo.

But he was certain that he didn't have a lot of time. He didn't know just how far Columbus was from Bremerton, but he guessed they'd be where they were going in another thirty minutes, maybe forty-five. And in the dark, he'd have to feel his way, whatever he chose to do.

He eased the door latch open and let himself out onto the truck bed's flat surface, holding onto the side of the car to keep from tripping. He bent low and crawled toward the front end. Trying to remember just how the vehicle was anchored, he felt along the worn bed until his hand bumped a heavy chain. That's right—when they'd put the car on, they must have anchored it with two chains at the front, two at the rear. He could certainly fix it so the car wouldn't roll.

He moved to the left front tire, felt around it until he located the valve stem, and worked his fingernail onto the small valve. He depressed it—and the sudden hiss of escaping air made more noise than he'd expected. Quickly, he released it and held himself perfectly still, waiting to see if the sound had attracted Charlie or Jake.

Nothing.

He pressed the valve again, holding it longer this time. And when he released it once more to listen for the men, he realized that it was impossible for them to hear anything he did unless it made more noise than the whistling wind and the roaring engine. Nodding to himself that he was safe, he proceeded to let all the air out of the tire.

Ten minutes later, feeling his way about the Mercedes, he had all four tires as flat as he could make them. As he felt about the final one, though, and discovered it was totally flat, he also realized that the vehicle was not as tight against its restraining chains as it had been. Letting out the air had loosened the anchors.

But when he touched the chains, he discovered that they still held firmly—the vehicle might shift forward and back, but it could move only inches.

Scott smiled to himself.

They'd have a hard time rolling it off unless they pumped up the tires first.

His hand slipped up and onto the hood and for a moment he thought he should raise it, feel about the engine, and disconnect all the wires he could locate. Trouble was, he didn't know how to release the hood, and he didn't have a light to help him find the catch. Well, there were wires under the instrument panel. He could get to those easily.

Working his way back to the door, he slipped inside once more and onto the seat. He bent over, stretched himself out, and felt all around. He touched one wire and jerked it loose. He touched two more and tugged at them until they gave. He found a bundle of them in one place, all taped together. He pulled as hard as he could, but this time nothing yielded.

Those, he just knew, were the main wires.

As he continued to feel about, his fingers discovered a flat, plastic surface. He stopped and thought hard, trying to remember something he had once heard his father say—something about fuses. He wasn't sure what they did, but he knew they had something to do with the vehicle's electric system.

Hey, now. Houses and fuse boxes. And he knew that if a fuse blew at any time, the lights went out, and they wouldn't come back on until a new fuse was screwed in place.

That's what the fuse box in a car was for. The fuses would be different, but they served the same purpose.

He ran his fingers over the plastic surface, felt for a small catch at its side, and found the little prongs that held fuses in place. He wasn't certain how to remove them, but he kept jiggling them until something gave.

He brought it up close and felt it carefully. He couldn't be certain, but it seemed to be a glass tube, thinner than a pencil and about an inch long, maybe less. He put his hand on the box again and kept pulling until he'd gotten all the fuses out. He had no idea what he was doing, but he believed that he was separating the battery from everything that depended on electricity—the ignition, the lights, the starter, and even the radio.

When he finished with that bit of mischief, Scott sat up and took a deep breath. Now, what else could he do to slow them down when they began to move the Mercedes?

There was the gasoline tank—but he had no way of draining it. And besides, if they couldn't get the switch and starter to work, gasoline wouldn't make it go. If he could take off the steering wheel—

He was startled as the truck suddenly swerved toward the side of the road and slowed down. He slipped out of the car and hastened to the side of the stake bed to see what had happened. Cautiously, he lifted a corner of the tarpaulin.

Jimbo sniffed and wished he could wipe his nose. And he wished he could get all that leftover tape-goo off his cheeks and chin. It itched and felt like it was going to leave a permanent burn—or whatever that stuff did to skin. His mouth was dry, and he couldn't work up enough spit to moisten his tongue; every time he tried to move it around, it kept getting stuck to his teeth or to the roof of his mouth.

"You're both going to get caught—I guess you know that," he said. "I told you my daddy was chief—"

"Aw, shut up, kid," Jake said. "Your old man's not chief of anything."

"Well, my uncle is. He's with the FBI and don't think my daddy won't call him. You just wait and see. He'll call him as soon as he knows what happened to me and all the FBI will get you."

Charlie laughed. "Jake, we got us a toughie. Should have left him with Dave."

"Should have done lots of things except bring him along." Jake shifted and pushed Jimbo away from his side of the seat. "What are we going to do with him?"

"You'll see, once we get to Columbus."

Jimbo didn't like that kind of talk. He didn't want to let them think it, but he was frightened. He'd heard about how people like these two would do just about anything to kids—lock them in a car trunk and not tell anybody, put them in boxes and bury them with just a little air hole to breathe through.

He sniffed again. Well, maybe they *thought* they knew what they were going to do with him, but they were wrong. He meant to work himself free of the ropes, get his legs untied, too, and the very next time they stopped, even if it was just for a red light, he meant to leap over Jake and go out the window.

The idea made him concentrate on the rope that held his wrists, and he began again trying to work his fingers into the knot. He leaned forward, then shifted on the seat so his fingers could work freely.

And all of a sudden, something gave. He sat very still for a moment, then gradually extended his elbows toward Charlie and Jake. He coughed so their attention would not be on his arms and leaned back. There it went again, and this time he knew that his left hand wasn't as bound as it had been. He worked harder with his fingers, finally slipping one of them into the knot itself. He twisted and probed, twisted again, and deftly tugged.

The wrist slipped easily, and he caught himself just before the knot became completely untied. He started to bring a hand around but very quickly stopped the act. Couldn't let Charlie know.

He leaned forward just enough to give himself room, and while he kicked out with both legs, making his feet bump into the instrument panel, he worked the right arm free.

Now—now he could do something.

"Boy, don't kick the dashboard no more," Charlie said. "You could bust the speedometer or the switch."

"I don't care," Jimbo said. "I might just try to kick the doors off."

Jake laughed and lighted a cigarette. "Boy, you ain't about to kick nothin'—you hear me? Nothin'."

Jimbo had worked his arms free by moving them up and down, by slipping his fingers into the rope and tugging at the knot. He ought to be able to do the same with his feet, except that he couldn't get at the knot. But he could kick back and forth.

"Yeah?" He turned toward Charlie. "I can kick if I want to and nobody's going to stop me."

"Kid," Charlie said, "you're asking for a bash across the face."

"You hit me and my daddy'll really be mad." That's it, he told himself, get them thinking about one thing while he was working on another. "I don't care how far you run, if you hurt me, the FBI and my daddy'll catch up with you."

His ankles seemed to be separated more than they were five minutes earlier. The knot was slipping. Or maybe the rope was stretching, he didn't know for sure. But he could move one foot at least two inches, maybe three, from the other.

Just a little while longer and his feet would be free of the binds. They'd be free, and his arms would also be able to move. He could make a sudden grab for the blindfold and snatch it off, kick the gearshift, and make the truck stop. And while Charlie was trying to make it go forward again, he'd just scoot across dumb Jake, let himself through the window, and hit the ground running.

"How much longer?" Jake asked.

"Oh, forty-five minutes. Maybe an hour. Depends on traffic."

"We got no traffic here."

"I mean in Columbus."

The rope didn't fall from his ankles, but Jimbo knew that his legs were almost free. Just a little longer, and he'd have only the blindfold to think about.

"How long'll we have to stay in Columbus?" Jake asked.

"If Jeffrey has enough men, I don't guess we'll be there more'n half an hour. Maybe forty-five minutes." Charlie slowed down to wait for oncoming traffic before maneuvering around a slower-moving truck. "Grab a beer, and we'll be on to the Big A."

Cautiously, Jimbo moved his knees apart, hoping that Jake did not notice. Then he very slowly moved his right foot. He couldn't be certain, but he thought the rope had fallen off—it didn't feel as if anything touched his foot. He swallowed hard, then caught himself.

He had another idea.

Last year, just before school was out, he had had to take a spelling test and hadn't been able to remember some of the words. He'd swallowed hard, made a little sound, and before he'd known it, he had been gagging as if he were about to spit up. Miss Moses had been sure he was sick and had sent him out of the room. He'd gone to the boy's room and had remained there till he'd remembered how to spell "handicap."

Maybe Charlie and Jake would think he was sick if he did the same thing now.

Wouldn't hurt to try. And if he got their minds on that, it would be a lot easier to slip past Jake and run.

He swallowed once more, this time making a louder noise. He took a deep breath, touched his tongue to his lips, set his jaw, and got his throat busy.

The sound was just what he meant it to be—no, it was even better. He was hungry and his stomach was empty, and once he forced his throat to make the rumbling noise, his stomach began to growl and rumble.

"Hey! Kid, you gettin' sick?"

Jimbo stretched his neck forward, made his jaw work, swallowed hard, and forced himself to gag.

"Charlie! Better let 'im get to the side of the road. I don't want no brat spittin' up all over me!"

"Boy!" Charlie abruptly put on the brakes and slowed the truck to a near crawl. "You got to spit?"

Jimbo was now going through all sorts of motions. He made his body shake, he worked his jaw up and down, he moved his head forward and back, as if trying to swallow whatever he pretended to be tasting. But he didn't forget to nod vigorously.

Charlie found a wide shoulder. "Hold it—hold it, boy! Jake, open the door and get 'im out of here!"

Jake waited till the truck was still, then he quickly

91

pushed down the handle. He eased down, stepped to the side, and reached for Jimbo's arm. "Here, boy, I'll help you—"

Jimbo's right hand flew up. With a sudden, deft motion he jerked away the blindfold and threw it in Jake's face. "Don't need any help!" And before Jake could react, he sprang past the man and hit the ground rolling over.

"Dang kid!" Charlie yelled. "Grab him!"

Jake whirled about, tripped over an unseen rock, and went sprawling over the gravel. He cursed at Jimbo and scrambled to his feet, reaching for the boy as he did so.

Jimbo pushed Jake's arm away, bounced up, and yelled, "You're not going to take me anywhere!"

He took one quick step, then a second. And just as he fell again, he realized that although the ropes about his ankles had loosened, they had not fallen away but were still binding him. He sprawled on the hard surface, rolled over, and was frantically trying to push the last strand of the rope off his leg when Jake grabbed his shoulder. "Brat! Dumb little brat!"

Jimbo kicked and hit and pushed as hard as he could, but Jake's arms were more powerful than he had imagined. "Let me down! You big bully, let me go!"

Jake shoved him roughly into the cab once more, clamped a huge hand on his neck, and climbed in after him.

From his hidden vantage point, Scott watched as the

door banged open, watched as Jimbo scrambled out and fell to the ground, watched as Jake grabbed for him, lifted him as if he were a sack of potatoes, and flung him back into the cab.

And he knew, as the truck began moving forward once more, that they'd bind Jimbo tighter than ever, that they'd be watching his every move, and that whatever happened in Columbus, Jimbo would not be able to help. Whatever else, Scott knew, he'd have to concentrate on freeing Jimbo.

Chapter Ten

Ellie sat on the floor of the sheriff's office, off to the side of Deputy Long's desk. The young fawn was in the box the deputy had found for her, and Ellie was holding a plastic saucer of milk for it to drink from. Deputy Long had gotten some medicine and gauze as soon as he'd called a photographer to come in, and he'd helped her wipe the injury clean. "Not as bad as it looked," he'd said. "You just keep him still."

Five minutes later, the photographer, a young man with a bushy, red beard, had come in carrying two black cases about the size of portable typewriters. Deputy Long had told Ellie that Mr. Jernigan—that was the photographer's name—would process the film. Processing, she knew, meant developing them and making prints. But she didn't see how he could do it so quickly. Usually, back home, when she took a roll of film to be developed, she didn't get the pictures back for at least two days.

She had finished feeding the little animal, had encouraged it to lie down, and was stroking it gently when a back door opened. Mr. Jernigan came toward Deputy Long, holding half a dozen prints. Ellie sprang to look.

Deputy Long spread the prints on the desk top. "Pretty fair shots," he said.

Ellie leaned close and pointed to one of the blowups. "That's Jimbo," she said excitedly. "Look—look how they tied him up!"

Using a pencil-like pointer, Mr. Jernigan touched the area of the photograph that Ellie had pointed out. "He's gagged," he said.

"And they put him in the truck with that thing over his mouth!" Ellie turned to Deputy Long. "The police have to catch those men before—before—" but she didn't finish.

The deputy put a reassuring hand on her shoulder. "You said they were heading toward Columbus?"

"That's what I think they said. But I don't know where Columbus is."

"We do." Deputy Long shifted his attention to another picture, one showing the truck's rear. "Doug, can you make out the tag?"

The photographer bent over the picture and held a small magnifying glass over the back section of the truck. "I can get the letters. Looks like *RJH*. But the numerals are blurred."

95

"Painted over?"

"No—looks more like mud's caked on the plate."

"How about the truck itself—anything you can make out?"

The photographer studied that photograph and three others very carefully. "Nothing's clear. Could be a Dodge, could be a Chevy. Might even be a GMC."

"But one of those three?"

"Definitely one of those three."

Ellie picked up one of the pictures and turned it to the side to get it out of the light's direct glare. "Hey—I think these two are the men in the truck."

The deputy turned quickly. "Let's see."

She pointed to one of the men, the lower half of his body hidden by the truck's high fender. "This one's Charlie. I think that was his name. And this one," she pointed to a shorter man with thick hair, one hand on his hip, "this one's Jake."

Deputy Long touched another picture. "What about these two? Do you recognize them by any names?"

Ellie shook her head. "I heard somebody use the name 'Hunker' or something like that, and I heard 'Dave'—yeah, I'm sure it was Dave." She stared at the photo a moment longer, then faced Deputy Long. And as she stared up at him, tears suddenly welled up in her eyes. Now that she saw the pictures, she understood for the first time how real the danger was for Jimbo and Scott. "You'll call somebody to be on the lookout for them, won't you?"

The deputy nodded, but before he could answer, they both heard a whirring, swishing noise coming from the parking lot across the street. "That sounds like a 'copter." He ran toward the door.

Ellie waited a moment, then trotted after him.

It was a helicopter, and just as she reached the door to the small county courthouse, she saw a man and two women bending low as they moved out from under the still-turning rotor.

"It's—it's Aunt Louise!" And with a little cry, Ellie darted down the short flight of steps and across the narrow stretch of lawn, not stopping until she had crashed into her aunt.

Louise bent down and hugged her close. Tears were in her eyes. "Thank God you're safe," she said.

"I was scared, though. Real scared." Ellie pushed away. "But those men still have Jimbo—I just hope they haven't found Scott."

Alice Hamner turned quickly to her. "What about Scott?"

Ellie told them how she and Scott had climbed into the Mercedes, how they'd hidden there during the first part of the ride, and how Scott had tricked the men so she could get away. "It was sure a long walk, though."

Deputy Long met them and escorted the group back inside. Without wasting words, he led them to his desk and pointed out the pictures. He picked up the one with Charlie and Jake. "Ellie has identified these as the men taking the boys to Columbus."

Sheriff Blake studied them a moment. "The one called Jake's a stranger to me. But there's something about Charlie that looks familiar." He turned to the other pictures, quickly picked out the one showing the truck's rear end. "The tag—"

"Only the letters are clear, Sheriff," Mr. Jernigan said. He handed him the magnifying glass.

Sheriff Blake studied the photo a moment. "It's a Chevy." He pointed to a very tiny emblem attached to the license plate. "Bradly Marcus Chevrolet uses that." He studied the letters a moment longer. "Not much to go on, but maybe we can run a tracer. Mind?" He was pointing to the telephone.

"Go ahead," Deputy Long said.

The sheriff dialed a number, waited a moment, then said, "Harris, Blake here. . . . Yes, we're in Durango County. . . . Right, quick trip. . . . Yes, they've developed the pictures. . . . Right, now, tell Henley to run a file check on Charlie—that's right, Charlie . . . he's one of the men with the truck they told us about. . . . I can't put a last name to Charlie yet, but he's about six one, maybe one ninety, thick, black hair, and I think"—he reached for the photograph—"I'm pretty sure he has a small scar across his chin."

Ellie stood on tiptoe and studied the picture the sheriff held. "He *does* have a little scar—I remember it now."

"Now, something else . . . we can't get the full tag,

but the letters are RJH . . . a Chevy, two-and-a-half ton stake-bed . . . right."

Ellie caught Louise's hand and pointed to the small box over against the wall. "I wasn't all alone on my walk," she said. "I had company," and she led her aunt to the little fawn.

Louise bent down and gently touched the animal's head. Her hand moved softly to the bandage. "How'd you come to find it?"

Ellie told her. Then she told her about the man and woman at the mobile home. "I sure am glad I didn't go inside," she said. "I think that man would have killed Lucky—"

"Lucky?"

"That's what I call him," Ellie said, indicating the fawn. "He sure was lucky that whatever hit him didn't kill him."

"And lucky you picked him up," Louise said, giving her another light squeeze.

Alice joined them and bent over. "Ellie, was Scott hurt?"

"No, ma'am. And he's really strong—you should have seen him throw that hood thing over the truck side."

Alice patted her shoulder.

"But Jimbo's all tied up," Ellie said, her smile vanishing. "And blindfolded."

"Does he know Scott and you were on the truck?"

"No, ma'am."

". . . Yeah, that's right," the sheriff was saying. "What'd you find out? . . . Nobody answered at his home or business, hunh?"

Ellie wondered whom the sheriff meant and turned her attention to the telephone conversation.

". . . Hey, good, good!" Sheriff Blake turned and nodded to Deputy Long. "We may have a lead—" He cut short the comment and returned to the telephone. "A telephone number written on a pad?" He hesitated a moment, then turned to Ellie. "Did you hear any of the men mention where they were going?"

"Just to Columbus."

The sheriff turned back. "Right. Now, here's what you do . . . have the telephone company trace every call made from the trucking firm's office for the past ten hours. . . . Right, particularly any to Columbus . . . and get in touch with Chief Batson, Bremerton's city office. Ask his cooperation and get an All Points Bulletin out for Dave Ferguson. . . . I'm not certain, no, but I think he's up to his ears in this one."

As soon as the sheriff hung up the phone, Alice and Louise hurried to him. "Anything?"

"Harris talked to the highway patrol, but they think the truck slipped through. May already be out of the state by now. But I think we'll know the truck's destination in a short while."

"Ellie said Columbus—"

"I mean the specific place in Columbus," the sheriff said. "Somebody's expecting a delivery."

Ellie turned to him. "Are we going to Columbus?"

He smiled at her. "That won't be necessary. I've sent Captain Townsend to join with the Columbus police and the sheriff's department there." He glanced toward Louise and Alice. "There's nothing more we can do here."

"Sheriff," Deputy Long said, "how can we help?"

"You've helped already," Sheriff Blake said. He nodded toward Ellie. "Getting this young girl here, developing the pictures as you did—"

"You can thank Doug, here, for that."

"We do," the sheriff said.

Five minutes later, they were all aboard the helicopter for the flight back to Bremerton. Ellie sat in the smallest seat, cuddling Lucky in her arms. "I wish, I wish," she was saying slowly.

"What do you wish, honey?"

"That Scott and Jimbo were going home with us." She took a deep breath and stared out as the helicopter lifted off, made a half-circle over the parking lot and zoomed away west, toward Bremerton.

Chapter Eleven

Dave Ferguson paced back and forth between the edge of the highway and the parked pickup truck, near the Triangle Service Station's blacktop drive. Each time he reached the highway, he paused, shaded his eyes from the lights of passing automobiles, and stared off in the direction of his farm, half a mile away. And when he saw nothing, he muttered to himself.

After almost an hour of waiting, he spat on the ground and threw down the fourth cigarette he'd lighted. He crossed to the drink machine and jammed a quarter in the slot, hitting the side almost immediately because the selection was slow dropping from the automatic rack.

"Reckon he fell in one of them sinkholes?" Lou asked. He and the Lucas brothers were sitting on the tool boxes stacked in the pickup's small bed.

"He knows where they are," Dave said. "He was supposed to follow the path by the river."

"Might of got himself caught," Jamie Lucas said. "Tommy ain't never been too quiet about what he's doin'."

"I hope he's not caught," Dave said. He looked at them. "You'd all better hope not, too. But I don't intend spending the rest of the night waiting on him."

"Hey," Lou said suddenly. "Ain't that him yonder?"

Dave spun around. "Yeah—has to be."

Minutes later, Tommy joined them. "Man," he said. "Man!"

Dave faced him. "*What* took you so long?"

Tommy took a deep breath and glanced over his shoulder. "It's all burning," he said. "Cars, barn, maybe the house—"

"I said nothing about the house, stupid—"

Tommy grabbed his shoulder. "Don't call me stupid!"

"Okay, okay," Dave said. "But what took so long?"

"I done what you said—torched the place and throwed them bombs. And man," he smiled, "did they blow!"

"Yeah, yeah," Dave said. "We heard the fire truck. But man, that was forty-five minutes ago."

Tommy shook his head. "Dave, we got trouble."

"Like what?"

"Like—when them things exploded, that sheriff came charging across the field. Him and them others got out to look. And while they was lookin', his radio got to

103

squawking. I sneaked close as I could without nobody seeing me. You ain't going to like it."

"Like what, man! Like what?"

"You know about them others with the kid?"

"I know there was supposed to be somebody with him."

"There was two of 'em—"

"I already know that."

"Yeah, but what you don't know is, they was on the truck, too."

"Are you *sure*?"

Tommy nodded his head. "Reckon they must of slipped up onto the Mercedes or them parts while we wasn't looking. One of them—a girl, I think they said—jumped off somehow, and they got her in the Durango County sheriff's office now. And she's got pictures they mean to print—"

"Pictures?" Dave stared at him. "You sure?"

"I ain't sure of nothing except that's what they said." He also added that he understood the sheriff was going to Durango and that his deputy was heading for Columbus. "Looks like we've got us some real trouble."

Dave turned halfway and stared off in the direction of the farm. "They don't know everything—not yet."

"I reckon it won't take too long to find out," Tommy said. "If they got pictures of the truck, maybe of us—"

"You don't have to spell it out," Dave said abruptly. He thought for a moment. "Maybe you and the rest better disappear for a while."

"With what?" Tommy asked. "We got maybe five bucks between us."

Dave glanced at the others, who'd now gathered around him. "I'll go to the office and get money for all of you. Tommy, come along with me and bring it back to the rest."

Minutes later, Dave turned off the highway and started to park by his trucking office. Tommy nudged him. "Wait—look yonder."

At the parking area's far side, half-hidden by the building, Dave spotted the rear end of a sheriff's patrol car. He took a deep breath. "How? How'd they connect me?"

"I don't know," Tommy said, "but we won't be going in there."

Dave accelerated and drove past the building. Half a block beyond, he pulled off the road. "Get your car," he said, "but don't follow me. I've got some money at my place. I'll get it and meet you others—"

"We don't want to be sitting at that service station for an hour or so," Tommy interrupted.

"I won't be that long," Dave said. "But I'll meet you at Lenny's Burger Bar. Okay?"

"Okay," Tommy said slowly. "But make it soon."

Dave remained where he was, watching in the rearview mirror, until he saw Tommy slip past the patrol car, work his way to his Oldsmobile, and back out. Then he eased onto the highway and headed toward Bremerton's south side.

When he reached his apartment, Dave parked his pickup on a side street, away from the bright corner lights, and walked back. He stopped on the small stoop and looked all around the apartment parking lot, just to make sure he hadn't been followed, then let himself in. He walked through the living room, turned on the hall light, and made his way into his bedroom. Inside the wide closet, he unlocked the hidden safe and took from it all the cash he had. He counted it rapidly, discovering that he had a little more than ten thousand dollars on hand.

He closed the safe and stared at the rack of clothing a moment. Then he took down a worn briefcase and a large overnight bag from the closet shelf. He carefully placed the money in the smaller case, then packed the other with shirts, pants, and the necessities he thought he wanted.

When he was ready to depart, he turned off all the lights except for a small lamp in the living room. He turned on the television set, but only loud enough for it to be heard by someone at his door. Then he went out.

Leaving the pickup where he'd parked it, he crossed the lot and climbed into his small sedan. He started the motor, backed out, and eased onto the avenue. But he did not turn in the direction of the highway leading to Lenny's Burger Bar.

Twenty minutes later, Dave Ferguson pulled into the crowded parking lot of the Bremerton Municipal Airport. Pocketing the car keys, he hurried toward the well-lighted entrance. He checked three departing schedules before finding a flight that would leave within ten minutes. Its destination was Atlanta.

Chapter Twelve

Scott was hungry, tired, and a little sleepy. He wished he could wash his face, moisten his lips, maybe wet his eyes and make them stay open. He had no idea how far they'd driven, but he felt sure that they were almost to Columbus. And he still had not the slightest idea how he could help Jimbo.

He glanced toward the side—and sat up suddenly. Although he could not see beyond the tarpaulin, he was aware of light seeping under it, the kind of reflected flashes that told him they were in an area busier than the highway. The outskirts of Columbus, had to be. And in a little while, Charlie would reach the warehouse or storage lot where the Mercedes would be unloaded.

He smiled. Where they meant to unload it. But that would not be so easy.

The truck seemed to be going more slowly, and Scott

knew that meant more traffic. It also meant for sure that they were getting close to their destination. He opened the Mercedes door and climbed out. He didn't know how the unloading men would work, but once the truck stopped, he wouldn't have time to hide—he had to do it now.

He felt about until he located three large boxes stacked near the front of the truck bed. One of them seemed lighter than the others, so he cautiously slid it to one side. The space left wasn't much, but he thought he could crouch in it, then pull the box close enough to keep the men from seeing him.

Trying not to tip the boxes over, he eased through the small opening and worked himself into the corner of the stake bed nearest the side of the cab where Jake was sitting. He hunkered down, set his feet firmly against the heaviest box, then slowly pulled the other two closer. He made certain, however, that a small gap was kept free, just enough for him to peer through without being seen by whoever climbed aboard.

Scott leaned against the lattice-like side of the truck bed and forced himself to relax. To relax and think—he had to think now, while he still had a few minutes.

He'd told himself they'd either park inside the warehouse or in a large, fenced-in yard, but the more he thought about it, the surer he was that they'd be inside a building. Unloading a stolen automobile in the open, even at midnight, might attract the attention of someone driving by. Maybe even the police.

The truck began moving a bit faster, and Scott just knew they were not too far from where they intended to go. He'd have to make his move just as soon as they reached the place—that would be the only chance he'd have to slip off before the unloaders climbed on. But that was only a small fraction of what he'd have to do. He'd have to get the men's attention somewhere away from the truck, he'd have to get Jimbo untied, and they'd both have to run.

But how? How?

Scott shook his head, wishing he knew what the inside of the place they were going to looked like.

Although he was still unable to make out distinct shapes, Jimbo knew by the sounds along the road that they were getting into a busier area. Charlie had to slow down; more lights played across the windshield—Jimbo couldn't really tell where the lights were coming from, but the flashes across his face were more frequent.

He did not want to go where they meant to take him. He knew, he just knew, they'd be inside some big, dark building—maybe like the barn, except its sides would be concrete or brick, its doors would be heavy, and he wouldn't have any place to run and hide. His best chance was to get away from Charlie and Jake before they arrived at wherever they meant to leave the Mercedes.

He could pretend he was sick again—but no, they wouldn't buy that a second time. Likely, Jake would just put a hand on his knee, then bash him one across the face. He frowned and tried to think of another time when he got out of something.

Hey, at school.

Back when he was in the second grade and didn't want to go on the stage and sing by himself.

He'd started forward, then stopped and raised his hand, signaling frantically that he had to go to the bathroom. No matter what she might have thought, Miss Carlysle had nodded her head, and he'd gone scooting out of the small auditorium. He hadn't really needed to go, but once he had made up his mind, he'd had to go through with it.

Slowly, Jimbo began to squirm in his seat. He kept his head facing forward. And after several squirms, he shifted to the left, bumping Charlie. He shifted again, this time to the right, bumping Jake. He hesitated a moment, then began shifting once more, to the left, to the right, to the left again.

"Hey, kid," Jake growled, "what's eatin' you?"

Jimbo did not answer, just kept shifting and squirming.

"I said, what's with you, boy?"

Jimbo made a noise swallowing. "I—I think I've got to go."

Charlie glanced about. "Boy, you just hold it. Hold it, now."

"That's the trouble—I can't." Jimbo made the words come trembling out, as if he didn't want to say them. "I can't help it if I have to."

111

"You can wait."

Jimbo shook his head. "I can't, either. I have something wrong with my insides and when I have to go, I just have to—that's all."

"We'll be there in fifteen minutes."

He knew they were getting closer to their destination, but he meant not to let them take him there. "In fifteen minutes it'll be too late."

"Boy, don't you go wetting your britches."

"I—I don't want to." And now the words came crying out, as if he were on the verge of tears. "Can't you understand? It's not something I want to do. I just have to."

Jake looked across at Charlie. "What d'you think?"

"I think he'd better wait. Can't you wait, boy?"

"I don't even want to go—I *have* to," Jimbo said.

Charlie said something Jimbo didn't understand, but he gradually let the truck slow down. "I don't want him wetting the seat," he said. "There's a service station yonder."

"Boy, how come you didn't have to go when we could have got you into the bushes?"

"I don't decide when I have to," Jimbo said. "Don't you know *anything* about nature?"

Charlie let up on the gas, braked slightly, and gradually steered the truck into the service station. "Boy." his voice was low, controlled, and threatening. "Jake's going to take you to the restroom. And he's going to untie your arms and legs—"

"What about the blindfold?" Jake broke in.

"Yeah, that too—don't want any nosy people wonderin' what we're doin'. But boy," Charlie put his hand on Jimbo's thigh and squeezed it until Jimbo thought he was going to cry out, "you go in there, and you get it done, and you come right back out. Jake'll be at the door. You try anything, I'll bust your face for you."

Jimbo trembled all over. "Yes—yes, sir. I won't. It's just that I have to—"

"Yeah, yeah," Charlie said. "But you heard me. Don't try anything."

As Jimbo walked beside Jake toward the restroom, his small hand clutched tightly in the man's much larger one, he looked all around. Off to one side, he spotted three automobiles, one jacked up. Beyond it was a huge trash bin and a convenient telephone booth. In the other direction, he spotted three people sitting in an old sedan—they looked like they were drinking beer or something. But there wasn't one customer at the gas pumps. He'd hoped there'd be at least one—somebody he could holler to. He turned his attention to the station's small office, but didn't see anyone there. The attendant, he supposed, was in the service bay.

Well, he'd just have to do it without any help.

He got to the door and started in. Jake held him back. "Boy, I don't want any monkey business, you hear? You go in there and do what you have to, then you come right back out. Hear me?"

Jimbo nodded.

"I mean to wait right here, so don't try any funny stuff."

Again Jimbo nodded, now wiggling about as if he could not wait another minute. As soon as Jake released him, he pushed open the door and rushed inside. He took three steps, stopped, looked back to make sure the door was closing on its own, then tiptoed back to it. The moment it clicked shut, he turned the small lock in the doorknob. "Now, come get me if you can." But he didn't say it loud enough for Jake to hear.

He scurried through the small swinging doors, knowing there'd be a tiny window up high—something he could jump for. But there was no window. Except for the entrance, there was no other opening to the room. It was one solid stretch of four concrete block walls.

Jimbo took a deep breath and turned on the lavatory faucet. He kept twisting the knob until the water was running full force and splashing in the basin.

He waited a moment before he turned it off. Then he set it at a slow trickle.

He waited until he thought he heard somebody walk by outside. He took a deep breath, faced the door, and at the top of his voice yelled, "*Help!* Somebody help me!"

He listened. Nobody came to the door, nobody called to him.

"Help! I'm being kidnapped!"

Again he listened. The doorknob rattled, but instead of a stranger wanting to know what his trouble was,

114

Jake's low, growling voice demanded, "Kid, hush! I said shut up!"

Jimbo sniffed and looked at the knob, watching as it wiggled. He knew Jake was now aware of the fact that it was locked from the inside. "I'm not coming out and you can't get me."

"I said, unlock this thing, boy. You're not playing with kids now. If you don't unlock it, I'll bust it down."

"They'll arrest you."

"Kid, ain't nobody comin' to help you, so shut up and get out of there. And I mean right now."

"No."

The knob shook again. The door rattled against its frame, and Jimbo guessed Jake was trying to force his way through it. A heavy hand pounded it once, twice, three times. "Kid, if you don't open up *now*, I mean to tear you up!"

Jimbo trembled and backed against the wall.

The knob shook again. The door was pounded one more time. Then heavy footsteps were heard moving away. Jimbo took a deep breath, and a slow smile crossed his face. He's gone, he thought, Jake's gone and he'll get back in the truck and they'll go away and as soon as somebody comes—

"Yeah," it was Jake's voice once more, "the kid ain't too bright. Fact is, he's retarded."

Jimbo swallowed hard.

A second voice said, "You oughtn't of let him go in by

himself." A key was slipped into the lock. "I got enough to do, runnin' this station by myself t'night, without havin' to put up with some dumb kid."

"Yeah," Jake said, "I know and I'm sorry to call on you."

Jimbo understood what was happening, but he meant not to be taken to the truck again. "I'm being kidnapped!" he hollered, knowing somebody else could hear him. "They're kidnapping me and taking me to some place I don't want to go!"

"I guess we'll *have* to take him some place he don't want to go," Jake told the service station operator. "As soon as we get the truck unloaded, I'm taking him to his mama—and we'll just have to return him to that asylum again."

Jimbo frantically looked about the small room, hoping for a window that he'd missed before. The walls were still solid. He turned to the small partition dividing the closet from the rest of the room. He could climb up on it—

The door creaked and swung open. Jake charged in. Jimbo backed against the wall, pressed himself there, and as soon as Jake got close enough, he began to kick out, to flail away at the man's husky midsection.

"Boy!" Jake grabbed Jimbo's arm, his heavy fingers digging into the soft flesh. "I don't want to hurt you none, but I mean it—you come on with me."

Jimbo struggled against him, turning to the stranger standing in the door. He was a young man, maybe nineteen or twenty, wearing a soiled T-shirt, faded jeans, and a red bandanna about his thick, dirty blond hair. "He's not telling the truth!" Jimbo yelled. "I don't know him—he's not taking me to my mother! He's kidnapping me!"

Jake's hand was squeezing harder, his fingernails digging into Jimbo's arm. Jimbo tried to struggle free, but Jake lifted him partway off the ground, letting him dangle there with his feet barely touching the hard, concrete floor. "Now come on, boy, I ain't got all night. Soon's I unload them truck parts, me and you're going to your mama. You want to see your mama, don't you?" He put the other arm about Jimbo's waist and lifted him easily.

Jimbo tried to hit him with his free hand. "I don't want you to take me *anywhere!* You let me go!" He pushed against Jake's chest, then squirmed about to face the service station operator. "You've got to help me! You've got to!"

The young man looked at him a moment, the hint of a smile on his lips. "Just go on with your old man, kid," he said. "He's not hurting you—he's trying to help."

Jimbo tried to struggle a moment longer. Then he relaxed. His body slumped against Jake's, and his arms fell limply down. "He is really kidnapping me," he said. But the words came tight and soft and weak.

The attendant stopped smiling. "Yeah. Yeah, I know."

Jimbo let himself be carried back to the waiting truck. He did not fight the blindfold. He did not fight the tape being put over his mouth. And he had no struggle left in him as Jake once more bound his arms and legs with the rope.

As Charlie started the engine, put the truck into gear, and began easing away from the service station, Jimbo bowed his head. He choked back a sob that came from deep inside. He had told himself that he would not cry. He had kept himself awake throughout the long drive, trying to think of some way to get away from them. He had been certain for all the hours since they'd caught him that they could not hold him, once he started to get away. But now he knew better.

Whatever they meant to do, they'd do, and he could not stop them.

In his carefully planned hideaway, Scott was surprised when the truck slowed down and pulled onto the service station ramp. He'd been sure that the next stop would be the unloading place, and he was caught off guard when he heard the door open and Jake climb out. He gingerly turned, eased the tarpaulin to the side, and peeped through. Seeing Jimbo, now unbound and able to walk, he almost shouted out to him. But in the instant before the words came, he saw the sign—Arnold's Texaco—and he guessed immediately what was going on.

Scott watched the two disappear around the side of the building. After a few moments, he heard the muffled shouts from inside the building. He could not make out the words, but a short while later, Jake came back to the front, calling the attendant and asking for the keys to the restroom.

He knew then what Jimbo was trying.

The attendant came out of the small office, bringing a large ring of keys. "Okay, okay, mister," he said. "You oughtn't of let him go in by himself."

"Yeah, well," Jake said, "I reckon you're right. If I'd have known it'd be so he could lock it that way, I'd of never let him go in."

Scott turned so he could put one foot on the stake side. He could very easily climb up, jump off, run around to the other side of the service station, and before Charlie could do anything about it, he could hide—there had to be some place to hide back there. And once he got away, he'd go to the telephone, call the police, and tell them about the truck.

He shoved one of the boxes out of his way, set himself, and raised the edge of the tarpaulin. Easy. Over the side, drop down to the paved surface, scamper away. Nothing to it.

He set one foot firmly on the first board, braced himself, and pressed down.

The board made a loud, cracking noise and broke in the middle. His foot slipped off, and he bumped his elbow on a box. Instantly, he heard Charlie's door open and knew that the man had heard the noise. He ducked back and hastily threw the tarpaulin over the corner of the side, completely closing it again. Once more, he crouched behind the stack of boxes. He dared not move again.

Charlie's heavy footsteps told Scott the man was walking all around the truck, that he paused at the rear, then made his way along the opposite side. Scott swallowed and held his breath. He heard the corners of the tarpaulin being lifted, and he knew, he just knew, that Charlie was going to find him.

"What's the trouble?"

That was Jake's voice, and Scott supposed he was now returning to the truck with Jimbo.

"Heard something," Charlie said. "Just checking to see where it came from."

"Likely something shifted," Jake said. "I'm tired of this kid—how come we don't just throw him on the back with the stuff?"

"Haven't got time to tie him there," Charlie said.

Scott heard the driver walk around to his side and climb back in the cab. He took a deep breath but made an effort not to make a sound exhaling. Nothing left now—nothing more to do until they got to where they meant to unload the Mercedes.

He listened, but this time he heard no sound from Jimbo. It frightened him. He wondered if Jake had hit him, maybe knocked him unconscious. He didn't like it, but he knew there was nothing he could do. Not now.

Chapter Thirteen

The small, twin-engine airplane landed smoothly at the Columbus airport and taxied to the Visitors' Parking Ramp. As soon as the engines were stopped, the small door opened and Captain Townsend, Ralph Hamner, and Walter Parks climbed down. They had taken only a few steps when four men, three in uniform, hurried from the hangar and joined them. Captain Townsend stopped. "Lieutenant Ridgeway?"

The man in civilian clothes nodded, extended his hand. "You're Townsend—we were notified to meet you." He introduced one of the men as Lieutenant Jessup of the Columbus police and the other two as Deputies Kinnard and Hatfield of the Graceland County Sheriff's Department. "Your deputy—Harris, I believe —wants you on the phone," Lieutenant Ridgeway said, and pointed toward the hangar door.

Captain Townsend nodded and hurried inside. He picked up the telephone. "Harris—Townsend here. . . . Yeah, just landed . . . what've you got for us?" He waited a moment. "Good, good." He took a pencil from the desk top and jotted down a name. "How about that number again? Yeah, I'm ready . . . 555-6120. . . . Right, right. . . . Yes, Lieutenant Ridgeway and his people met us. . . . We'll get a trace. . . . Good work, and what about the sheriff?" He paused. "Right, fine, fine." He paused again, then added, "Right, we'll get on it right away. . . . Yeah, I'll give them the word."

He hung up and returned to the others. He quickly introduced Ralph and Walter, then glanced at them. "Harris said the sheriff and your wives are with the girl—"

"That's a relief," Walter said. "Is she all right?"

"She is. And they got good pictures."

"Of the people?"

"Of the people," Townsend repeated. "And they've got Dave Ferguson tied into this mess."

"He's the one who said he hadn't seen—" Walter caught himself. "And he knows where the boys are!"

"Yes," Townsend said. "But they haven't gotten Ferguson."

"Can't they arrest him?"

The captain told him about the All Points Bulletin. "He must have gotten suspicious—something alarmed him, anyway. He is skipping out."

"How do you know that?"

122

"An off-duty policeman was at the ticket office of the Bremerton Airport parking lot—moonlighting, I guess —and he spotted Ferguson's car. The fellow left it in such a hurry he forgot to turn off his lights. Anyway, Harris checked the ticket desks—seems our Mr. Ferguson caught a plane for Atlanta."

"And?" Walter asked.

"And the Atlanta police will be at the airport when his plane arrives."

"Why can't they radio the pilot, have him ask Ferguson where the truck's taking our boys?" Ralph asked.

"We want to take him by surprise. Anyway," and Captain Townsend waved the slip of paper with the phone number on it, "it won't be necessary." He turned to Lieutenant Ridgeway. "If you don't mind, how about having your people trace this Columbus telephone number? We think it's the destination."

"Right," and without waiting, the officer hurried back inside the small hangar office. Five minutes later, he rejoined the group. "Got it," he said. "That number is in an old shipping warehouse south of the city—on Big Crescent Boulevard."

"Do you know the place?" Captain Townsend asked.

"I do. The old Atlantic and Gulf Transport Company used it as a secondary storage plant before they moved out of the city. It's about fifteen miles from here."

"Good, good," Townsend said. "We'll head out there right away." He turned to Ralph and Walter. "I don't think you two should make the trip—"

"We mean to," Ralph interrupted.

"We don't know what we'll be running into."

"They're our sons," Walter said quietly. "But don't worry—we'll stay in the car out of your way."

Captain Townsend hesitated a moment, looking first at one father, then at the other. "I'd feel the same," he said. He turned, then, to the lieutenant. "We're ready to move out when you are."

"Right," and the lieutenant led them toward two waiting vehicles. "The warehouse is out of the city limits, but Sheriff Morris has a backup team waiting to join us if necessary."

The young officer identified as Deputy Kinnard stopped as he was about to climb into his unmarked cruiser. "Lieutenant, I'll radio for assistance, but where do you want them to meet us?"

"You know the area better—use your judgment."

The deputy hesitated a moment. "How about the parking lot just south of the Graceland Shopping Mall?"

"Sounds good," the lieutenant said. "But ask for unmarked cars."

"Will do."

Walter and Ralph watched as the other vehicle moved away, then they climbed into the Columbus city patrol car with Captain Townsend and Lieutenant Ridgeway.

"Mr. Parks, Mr. Hamner," the lieutenant said as they moved out, "if the boys are on the truck, rest assured that our men will see that they're not harmed. They can handle these things. You can count on it."

"We do," Ralph said. Walter nodded in agreement.

The stake-bed truck came to an almost dead stop, as if waiting for oncoming traffic to clear, then it was maneuvered into a hard left turn. The front wheels bumped over what Scott suspected was a low curbing, and the car parts aboard the truck were jostled. The Mercedes rocked slightly but did not move forward or back. One of the boxes tipped toward him, and Scott hastily caught it to keep himself well hidden. The truck swung about, halted abruptly, then began backing up. It stopped after moving only a few feet, and he heard footsteps rapidly crossing concrete.

"Hey, are you from Ferguson?" The voice was kept low, but Scott was able to make out all the words.

"Right—got a Mercedes for you."

"Yeah, right. Hold it while we get the door open."

Scott crouched as low as he could, knowing the boxes shielded him from the rear gate, but wondering if he could be seen through the stake bed's open sides when the tarpaulin was removed. He moved back as close as possible to the cab of the truck.

Grinding noises told him that a heavy door was being raised, and he felt sure by the sound of it that an electric motor was operating it. The noise shuddered to a stop, and Charlie accelerated as he reversed the truck. The vehicle bumped over a rut or thick, concrete sill—Scott couldn't tell which—then moved on. He guessed it went twice its length inside the building before stopping.

Both truck doors opened, and only one of them shut—the one on Charlie's side. Charlie got out, and Scott heard Jake walking around the front of the truck.

"What kept you?" That voice came from the man who'd met them first.

"Dumb kid," Charlie said. "Should have let Dave handle him."

"Yeah—well, what does he expect us to do with him?"

"Whatever," Charlie said. "I don't care—just get him off my hands."

"What about the others?"

"What others? I don't know anything about any others."

Scott swallowed and tried to slide down farther behind the boxes. They knew about him and Ellie. Or did they? Were they only guessing because Charlie had called and told that Dave guy about the pictures?

"All I know is," the man said, "Ferguson wants you to call him."

"Did he say at home or the office?"

"He didn't say."

"Okay—but I want that Mercedes off the truck like right now. I've still got to make it to the Big A City."

Big A City, Scott thought. Atlanta—that's what the people on the CB called it.

"We'll do it soon's my men come back—"

"They was supposed to be waitin' on us."

"They got tired of waiting and ran up the street for coffee. Be back shortly."

"Well, I want—"

Scott didn't hear the rest because a door shut and cut off whatever Charlie was saying. The man, Charlie, and Jake had gone inside a small office—he guessed it was an office—Scott listened intently, but he couldn't hear anything. Good, good—right now was the time he had to act.

He eased the tarpaulin to the side, cautiously stuck his head out, and looked all around. The small lights gave a shadowy appearance to the huge room, but he could see well enough to make out a row of oil drums off to the side, an uneven stack of battered crates close to the office wall, and big, expensive automobiles parked at the opposite end of the warehouse. They had been recently painted—the smell was still in the air.

He slid himself almost over the side. There, he paused once more and scanned the office wall. A large window looked out into the warehouse, but a tattered piece of brown paper had been taped over it so that anyone in the little room could not be seen. And could not see him, he thought. The windowless door was closed.

Cautiously, he eased himself down. He hit the concrete, held his breath, and listened to make certain his little scraping noises had not attracted the men's attention. The office door did not move.

Keeping low, Scott worked his way around the side of the truck to Jake's door, stood once to make certain he'd still not attracted the men's attention, then very gingerly turned the handle.

Although he was still blindfolded, Jimbo turned suddenly at the sound. Scott opened the door, stepped up, and quickly put his hand over his friend's mouth.

"Bop u do?" The words came out jumbled, but Scott knew Jimbo was trying to ask "What are you doing?"

"Shhh, Jimbo—don't you make a sound—don't say *anything*."

Jimbo's head bobbed vigorously.

Scott removed his hand and pulled off the tape over Jimbo's mouth. "I rode in the back," he said quickly.

"Ellie—"

"She jumped off one of the times the truck stopped."

"They're going to do something bad—"

"Shhh," Scott cautioned once more. He reached up and deftly untied the blindfold. "Now," he whispered, "turn around so I can untie your hands."

"I don't like being here," Jimbo said. "Did you know I tried to get away two times—hey, where were you?"

"On the truck," Scott said. "But be quiet—they'll be back soon, and we don't want them to get us."

"I'd like to kick that big, fat Jake in the stomach—he's a real bully—"

"Shhh," Scott warned again.

"Okay, okay," Jimbo hissed, "but I sure would like to shush him one time."

Scott untied the rope binding Jimbo's wrists; then while his friend was rubbing circulation back into his hands, he turned his attention to the ropes around the ankles. "Did your feet go to sleep?"

"Everything went to sleep," Jimbo whispered. "My face hurts where the tape was stuck on, and my head hurts from that blindfold—just wait, I'll get even."

"I said shhh," Scott said. "Now, wiggle your ankles."

"They're numb."

"Well, try—try hard. We can't stay here."

Moments later, Jimbo held out one foot, then the other, working both ankles. "They still hurt, but they're not asleep now."

"Okay—come on."

Jimbo slid down, and the two crept around the rear of the truck, bending low, even though neither was tall enough to be seen over the loaded bed. They stopped when they were about to break from the shelter.

"Where'd Ellie go?" Jimbo asked.

"I don't know," Scott whispered. "She was going to look for a telephone."

"I bet she got lost. She doesn't know anything about this part of the country."

"But she's pretty smart," Scott said. "She'll find somebody."

"If she didn't get lost," Jimbo said.

Scott glanced once toward the office and saw that its door was still closed. "Come on—let's get behind those automobiles."

"How about those boxes—they're closer."

"I'm betting there's a door at the other end," Scott said. "Maybe we can hide and slip out."

"Okay—but I still want to bop that Jake a good one."

"You don't want to get caught again, do you?"

"They won't catch *me* again," Jimbo said.

They slipped hurriedly past the scattered boxes and cartons, eased around a huge post that seemed to help support the roof, and reached the safety of the two newly painted automobiles. They were just squatting down when they heard the office door open.

"It don't make sense," Charlie was saying. "If he wanted me to call, how come he didn't wait around?"

"Likely he got tired of waiting," Jake said. "But I don't believe them other kids got on the truck. We'd of seen 'em."

"Maybe," Charlie said. "But what about that hood that fell off? Maybe it didn't fall. Maybe it got throwed off."

Scott and Jimbo raised themselves up just enough to see through the windows of one of the automobiles. Jake and the man who'd been waiting for them were taking the tarpaulin off the truck. They carelessly piled it beside the truck, and Jake jumped aboard. Scott couldn't make out everything he did, but Jake seemed to be surveying the contents. He moved along the side of the Mercedes, paused, then whirled about. "Charlie! Come here and look—*who* did this?"

"Did what?"

"The tires is flat as they can be."

The third man stepped forward and peered at the vehicle. "Man, there's no way that thing'll roll—all of 'em flat."

Charlie looked, then turned to Jake. "Those other

kids—Dave must have been right. But if they were on this thing, where'd they go?"

"Likely they hopped off when you stopped to call Dave," Jake said.

"Maybe," Charlie said. He hurried around to the side of the truck where Jake had been sitting. "*Jake!*"

"Yeah? What now?"

"The kid—he ain't here!"

"That little dummy!" Jake jumped down, walked all around the truck, then stared off toward the boxes. "All right, kid, ain't no way you can get them ropes off. Maybe you can hop, but you sure can't run. Just show yourself."

Jimbo nudged Scott. "We got him fooled."

Scott nodded and hastily looked at the wall. He didn't see the door he'd hoped to find, but a crack in the corner suggested that it was there. The trouble was, between the corner and their hiding place behind the automobiles, there was nothing but open space. He wasn't too good at judging distances, but he guessed it had to be at least forty feet. As soon as they tried to run over there, Charlie and Jake and that other man would see them—

Something there moved.

Both Scott and Jimbo spun about, crouching. Scott had been right—there was a door in the corner. And as they watched, it opened. The two others who'd gone for coffee were returning.

Jimbo ducked as low as he could and hugged the side of the automobile. Scott did likewise.

131

The men had opened the door outward and stepped inside. The door came back partially, but did not close all the way.

"Hey, guys," one of the newcomers called. "What's happenin'?"

"It's that kid they brought with 'em." That, Scott knew, was the man who'd been waiting. "He got out of the truck, but he's hiding somewhere."

The newcomer laughed. "No place to hide—he's got to be behind those boxes, behind the drums, or"—he turned and jerked a thumb toward the painted automobiles—"there." He and his companion joined the other three.

"Boy!" That was Charlie. "I said, boy, you might as well say where you are—ain't no way you can get out of here, tied up like you are."

Jimbo nudged Scott. "I wish I could kick *him* in the stomach, too," he whispered.

Scott frantically looked all around, not knowing what he was searching for. He spotted a small table with tools scattered on it, a large air compressor, a paint sprayer, two large cans of either paint or oil—he couldn't be sure which—and three boxes of bolts and screws. But nothing to hit with, nothing to use for their defense.

But wait. Wait, now. Those boxes of screws and bolts—maybe if he and Jimbo got them and threw them a fistful at a time, they'd cause the men to dodge and jump about. And while they were occupied, he and Jimbo could make a dash for the door.

But maybe they couldn't throw that far. And maybe if they did, the men would come after them, anyway, catch them—

The oil, though, and the paint sprayer.

An idea came suddenly to him.

Charlie and Jake moved toward the scattered stacks of boxes, kicking them about as they searched for Jimbo. The other three moved toward the big drums. "Boy," Jake hollered, "we ain't got all night—now you might as well come on out, wherever you are, ain't no way you can run."

Scott touched Jimbo's arm, pointed to the bolts. "You grab those as soon as I say—just get a handful at a time and start throwing at them."

"What're you going to do?" Jimbo whispered back.

Scott pointed at the cans of oil and the sprayer. "We'll dump that oil on the floor—I saw it on TV once. And when they try to run across it, they'll fall flat."

"Maybe," Jimbo whispered, but he didn't sound convinced. "And that thing?" He pointed to the sprayer.

"I'll show you," Scott whispered back.

"Why can't we just stay here? They can't see us."

"They've got all night, and they won't miss this place." Scott pointed to the door. "We'll get them busy dodging and sliding, then we can run for it."

Jimbo hesitated a moment, glancing from the boxes of bolts to the door and back. "I don't like it—"

"You want to get away, don't you?"

"Yeah. But first, I want to get even with that Jake."

"All right. Hit him first if you want to."

"Now?"

"Wait—wait till they're all close together." Scott peered out of their hiding place. "Give me a second, then grab the bolts."

"Okay, but I don't like it."

"Like it," Scott said. "And aim like you were pitching a baseball."

"I mean to," Jimbo said. "Just you listen to old Jake holler."

Cautiously, Scott crawled from the freshly painted automobiles to the buckets of oil, pausing once to look at the sprayer and spot the switch. He caught the handle of one bucket, lifted it, and turned about. As he did so, his foot caught on a pipe he'd not seen and knocked it against one of the automobiles.

At the noise, all five of the men whirled about. "Hey!" Jake started charging in their direction. "The kid's got that far!"

"Now!" Scott said.

Without further urging, Jimbo grabbed a handful of the bolts, rose suddenly, and hurled them at Jake. One of them must have caught him in the face because he let out a loud yell, stopped abruptly, and began clawing at his cheek. Jimbo didn't wait to see what had happened, but grabbed another handful of bolts and hurled it wildly at all of the men.

The surprise of their attack made the men stop, as if waiting for another shower of bolts. That moment gave

Scott time to step out from behind the automobiles, aim the bucket of oil, and slosh it across the floor. Without waiting to see what its effect was, he grabbed the second bucket and sloshed it, too.

One of the newcomers took a step forward, slipped in the goo, looked for a moment like an ice skater who didn't know how to skate, and fell flat on his back. Charlie tried to keep his feet, but as soon as his left shoe hit the oil, he too went sprawling.

"Dummies!" and Jimbo threw bolts and screws again, this time making certain that he aimed for Jake.

In that little time, Scott whirled around, hit the switch that turned on the paint sprayer, and grabbed the nozzle. He'd never used one before, but he'd handled a garden hose and this didn't seem to be much different. He aimed it toward all five, squeezed the trigger—and sent a mist of green paint all over them.

"Hey, you brat!" But the man who'd met Charlie and Jake was suddenly busy throwing his arms up to keep the paint from his face and seemed to forget that he was supposed to chase the boys.

"Now!" Scott yelled. "Now—let's go!"

Jimbo ran to the door and held it open while Scott backed toward him, keeping the spray aimed at the five. He did not stop until he was standing in the open space. He put one foot halfway out, paused, aimed the paint toward Charlie, who was now crawling toward him, and squeezed the trigger as hard as he could. The fine mist abruptly became a thick, hoselike stream, and it caught

135

Charlie on the side of his head, sending paint all over his face and into his eyes.

Charlie stopped crawling, screamed, and held out a hand, trying to ward off the attack.

"I wish that'd been Jake," Jimbo said. "Give me the sprayer and I'll get him—"

"No," Scott said quickly. "Let's go while they're on the floor."

Together they scampered out and into the darkness.

"They'll still come after us," Jimbo said.

"Not if we can block the door," Scott said. He spotted an oil-soaked, four-by-four post that must have been used to prop up an automobile. "Let's get it!"

Together, they lifted the post, dragged it to the door, and propped it against the huge knob. Both of them stood on the post's other end, forcing it into the softer ground at the edge of the blacktop.

"Now let 'em try to come out!" Jimbo said.

"Yeah, but there's still the big door," Scott said. "The one Charlie drove through."

"It's electric, I think," Jimbo said.

"I know. Come on."

Together, they ran to the rear of the building. Scott slowed down, kicking bits of waste metal and lengths of wire out of his way. "There's got to be a—what do you call them?—meter box somewhere. You know, one of those things where electricity comes to houses."

"Hey, yeah—and if it's like the one at home, it's got a lever you pull to cut off the electricity," Jimbo said.

"Dad's always using it when he wants to work on the air conditioner and stuff."

"Let's find it fast," Scott said, "before they can turn on the door."

They scrambled over bent automobile fenders, old bumpers, discarded tires and wheels, all the while searching along the wall for the master current-switch. Scott worked his way around a rusting engine and was about to push aside an old, bent door, when Jimbo stopped suddenly and pointed up. "Is that it?"

Scott looked. "Hey—yeah, it's got to be."

The two scrambled toward the gray box and, as they'd hoped, found it to have a large handle. Scott reached for it.

"Don't get shocked," Jimbo warned.

"It won't shock me," Scott said. "It's insulated. We just have to watch out for wires." He caught the handle, pushed it, found that it wouldn't go up, and jerked it down. "Got it!"

"Boy, I bet old Jake's mad at me now," Jimbo said. "If we'd had time, I'd have squirted that paint all over him. Big dummy!"

"Come on," Scott urged. "Maybe they're in the dark now, but one of them'll find a flashlight, and they'll get that other door open."

"Yeah, and they'll come after us for *sure*," Jimbo said.

Keeping low, just in case somebody might have already gotten outside, they crept along the wall and out toward the main road. At the building's farthest corner they paused and looked back. "I don't see anybody," Jimbo said.

"Guess they're still trying to find their way," Scott said. "Come on."

They worked themselves around a parked automobile, glanced over their shoulders one more time, then headed for the sidewalk—and ran headlong into a very tall man!

Chapter Fourteen

"Were you scared?"

"I guess I *was* scared," Jimbo said. "I mean, that guy was bigger than anybody I ever saw before." He glanced at Scott. "Shoot, I bet he could have played linebacker for the Cowboys or the Steelers."

"Or the Redskins," Scott added.

"Yeah, *anybody*. And when he closed those big ham-hook fists of his on our shoulders, I just about died right there. But I wasn't too scared to kick—that's what I was about to do, too, till he put his finger to his lips and told us to shhh."

On that sunny afternoon, Ellie, Scott, and Jimbo were once more together, once more taking pictures. This time, however, they were gathered in the Hamners' backyard, watching as Lucky limped about and paused now and again to lick Ellie's hand.

"That was something," Scott said. "We thought we were all by ourselves—running away from Charlie and Jake. Shoot, I didn't have any idea that Sheriff Blake had sent people to join with the Columbus police—I still don't know how they got there so fast."

"They flew," Ellie said. "Like I flew in the helicopter from that place in—you know—"

"Durango County," Scott supplied.

"Yeah. That was something else." Ellie pointed to Lucky. "It didn't scare her a bit."

"Deers don't get scared like people do," Jimbo said.

"It's deer," Ellie said. "Singular or plural, it's all the same word."

Jimbo made a face. "I don't care. School's out, and if I say *deers,* I don't want any teacher telling me that's wrong."

"Okay, okay," Ellie said. She put her hand out, let Lucky lick her fingers, then gently caught the little animal and brought it close.

Jimbo watched for a moment, then laughed. "Yeah, it was something—we got out there and all of a sudden deputy sheriffs and plainclothes policemen were popping up from everywhere. The place was really surrounded."

"I wish I'd had my camera ready," Scott said. "I sure would have taken a picture of Charlie and Jake and those others. "He turned to Ellie. "They couldn't get out of that place till the police switched the power back on.

And they came out in handcuffs, with their faces all painted and stuff on their clothes."

Jimbo nudged him. "Did you see that look Jake gave me? Man, I bet he'd have choked me if he could have gotten his hands loose."

Scott leaned back against a small oak tree and watched Lucky. "That Lieutenant Ridgeway didn't believe it. All they had to do was bring the men out—Jimbo and I had done all the capturing."

Ellie looked up. "What about that Mr. Ferguson or whatever his name is?"

"He was *really* dumb," Jimbo said. "Running out on his buddies, catching an airplane to Atlanta like he could get away from the police. Shoot." He bent over and plucked a blade of grass. "*Anybody* ought to know better than to catch an airplane when police are after him." He caught himself and looked across at Ellie. "See there? I said *anybody* and *him*—is that good English?"

Ellie nodded. "But don't call me a teacher—it's summer."

Scott glanced up at the thick layers of limbs and leaves, recalling the details of their experience. The Columbus and Graceland County officers had come to the warehouse, had silently surrounded it, and were ready to move in when he and Jimbo got out. Of course, he'd had no way of knowing about them—as far as he knew, it was all up to him and Jimbo to get away on their own. But was he ever glad to see his father! He and Mr.

Parks had been in one of the patrol cars, but as soon as the men had seen their sons, they had bounded out and come running.

"Hey, Scott," Jimbo said.

Scott shook his head and turned to his friend. "Yeah?"

"You know what they say about Miss Youngblood?" Miss Nancy Youngblood would be their teacher when they returned to school in September.

"I know they say a lot."

"I mean about her asking everybody to write an essay about something they did in the summer. Boy, have we got one to write!"

Scott waved a hand. "That's three weeks off—don't talk to me about school."

Ellie cuddled Lucky and turned to her companions. "I'll write about how I found this cute little fawn."

"That ought to be good—not many people ever get to do that," Jimbo said.

Scott rose slowly and crossed to where Ellie was. He bent down and tenderly stroked the creature's head and neck. "The vet said he'd be all right—"

"It's a *she*," Ellie corrected.

"All right, she, then," Scott said. "*She*'ll be all right in a couple or three days."

"I know," Ellie said softly. "We can keep her that long, then the man from that game preserve'll come take her back to the woods."

"Yeah," Jimbo said, "but he won't turn *her* loose for a

while. He'll just let her grow till she'll be safe when she's free."

"I sort of wish we could keep her," Ellie said. "But it wouldn't be fair. She's a wild animal, and nobody has the right to keep her in a pen."

"They won't," Scott said. "But we'll have pictures."

"Yeah, and I'm glad."

Scott advanced the film in his camera, moved about four feet from Ellie, aimed, and snapped twice.

"One thing I won't ever forget," Ellie said as she released the animal and watched it walk slowly toward Jimbo. "I won't forget that woman and her blind husband. I guess I ought to write a letter to them—but I didn't get their names."

"Mom did," Jimbo said. "I think I heard her tell Pop it was Wissinger—something like that."

"Well, I sure want to write them a letter—maybe even send them my picture."

"And I mean to write that Lieutenant Ridgeway," Scott said. "He was nice—catching those crooks and sending us to the airport in that cruiser."

"Yeah—well, I'm going to write somebody, too," Jimbo said.

Ellie and Scott looked at him. "Who?"

"Jake!"

"*Jake?*" they both said in unison.

"Yeah," Jimbo said, smiling. "I'm going to write him in jail—and do you know what I'm going to tell him?" He glanced from Scott to Ellie and back. "I'm going to tell him 'Yah, yah, yah, you big, fat dummy!' How's that?"

Scott glanced at Ellie. She looked back at him. And all three of them laughed.